Dope Girl 5

Sa'id Salaam

Published by Black Ink Publications, 2020.

DOPE GIRL 5

First edition. April 13, 2020.

Written by Sa'id Salaam.

"Triggaaaa!" Cameisha wailed and pounded the steering wheel as she drove. She could still feel the spray of glass and blood from when Bilal shot him.

To add insult to injury, he'd killed himself before she could do it. She had no idea how or why they were even there. To make matters worse, she'd killed a cop. Her life was over and she knew it so she planned to take as many of her enemies with her as possible.

She and Trigga couldn't be together in life so she would join him in death. The recent memory of slitting Mama Salazar's throat almost broke through the mask of murder on her face. Juan and the rest of the family were on her list too, but not before...

"Fuckin' Dasia!" she growled. The very mention of the traitor's name made her foot heavy. She mashed the gas and sped towards St. Louis as her phone buzzed incessantly until it became annoying. Not having shit to talk about caused her to toss it in the backseat.

"Shit, Cameisha, answer the damn phone!" Samantha griped and tried calling again. Getting her voicemail once again, she finally decided to leave a message, "Girl, Trigga is alive! He's in ICU, but alive!"

****

"Come on, handsome," Nurse Brown encouraged as she changed Trigga's bandage. He was just barely clinging to life after having surgery to remove a bullet from his head.

If you had to get shot in the head, Atlanta was the city to do it in. The busy metropolitan area was violent enough to make the surgeons at Grady Memorial Hospital some of the best in the world. They specialized in gunshot wounds and gave him a fighting chance. Great news since chances of getting shot in the head are high in Atlanta.

"Lucky fellow," the doctor said since he didn't believe in God. He attributed good fortune to skill or luck. "Doubt if he'll ever be able to see again, but he should pull through."

Nurse Brown was too busy praying to reply. She prayed for all the men and boys who came in fighting for their lives. Lives that were often cut short over drugs, money and pussy. Her own son had lost this very same battle so she prayed extra hard so no more mothers would have to go through what she went through.

****

Cameisha ignored the rumbling plea of her empty stomach as she sped west. A traffic stop would have ended in a shootout because she had no plans on going down peacefully. She would gladly take death in the streets over life in the pen.

It would have taken too much of her borrowed time to stop and use the bathroom so she peed her pants. Her burning rage prevented the warm pee from even registering. She needed Dasia dead so she could get back to Atlanta. She had a funeral to attend.

"Damn!" Cameisha frowned as she pulled into the rundown motel's parking lot. She double checked the address and shook her head. Dope fiends scurried about like forest creatures.

Her mind flashed back to when she was a little girl. A baby possum had played dead and bit the shit out of her. It was a valuable lesson but her mind was too convoluted with hate to process it at the moment.

A car next to her stole her thoughts when the door opened. She watched curiously as a skinny addict leaned her big head out and spit out a mouthful of cum. The happy customer could now go home to his wife satisfied; albeit twenty dollars lighter. The addict got out and looked right through Cameisha. She didn't even register her because she was so focused on her next fix.

"Dasia?" Cameisha asked aloud to be heard over her own heartbreak. She got out and followed her into the rundown room. The funk of blood, ass and cum assaulted her nostrils when she stepped inside.

Lisa was on her knees with a john vigorously humping her face. She waved to be polite as Dasia went for the works to fix up her next fix. Lisa clamped down when she felt the spasms of an orgasm in her mouth. She swallowed with a loud gulp and pushed the john away. In a flash she was beside Dasia, ready to share the same dirty needle.

"Damn, I shoulda got you!" the trick said when he saw Cameisha standing in the doorway. He would never know how close he'd come to being murdered just then. The thought of Cameisha sucking some random cock almost got him shot.

Cameisha shook off the vision of shooting him in his face and looked at the sorry sight of her once good friend. She watched in horror as she frantically fixed up a dose of heroin. Lisa tied off her arm and looked up.

"What are you doing here?" she demanded. Even in her current state, she was still possessive and jealous over Dasia. "She's mine! Mine, you hear?!"

"I hear," Cameisha said and fired a shot right into her forehead.

Lisa leaned against the wall with a shocked expression on her dirty face.

Dasia looked up and tried to figure out what was going on. She frowned at Cameisha, trying to recall her face. A faint smile appeared when she got it. "I'm so happy to see you!" Dasia sighed in utter exhaustion. The life of an addict is a hard one. She would go days without sleep then sleep for days. She had been beaten up, raped and robbed more times than she could count. Death would be a relief.

"You...are?" Cameisha asked. She actually looked at her hand to make sure the gun was still there. It was, so why was she happy to see her? A warm tear ran down her face and into her mouth as she looked at her one-time friend.

"Gurl, yes! What took you so long? I'm ready to go," she said in relief. She lowered her head and spoke what she thought would be her last words. "I love you, Meisha-Meisha."

"I love you, too," Cameisha vowed as she raised the gun once more. She lined the three dot sight on a nasty bump on Dasia's forehead and began to slowly squeeze the trigger. "I can't!"

Dasia heard her friend's sobs and wails and lifted her head. Cameisha broke down and bawled like a baby. She got up and went over to comfort her.

"It's okay, Meisha. It has to be done. I violated, I deserve it."

"Yeah, you do, but I can't. I just can't," Meisha sobbed. "My Trigga is dead. I killed a cop. I killed Juan's mama. I'm dead, too. There's no way out!"

"Yes, there is! Where there's life, there's hope. I'm the one who's dead! I'm pregnant, by God only knows who. I got HIV, STDs and SUVs."

"SUVs?" Cameisha asked.

"Shit, I got everything else! Please, please put me out of my misery. If I kill myself, I ain't got no chance at going to heaven. I've had enough hell," she pleaded. Her life was bad but nowhere near as bad as hell.

Suddenly, the little possum popped back in her mind and caused a smile to spread on her face. She got it. Play possum. Play dead so that she could live. Just like her Dope Boy daddy.

"Come on, yo," she demanded.

"Where we going?" Dasia asked as she followed her from the room.

"Atlanta. I got a plan!"

Chapter 2

Cameisha stole glances at Dasia, asleep in the passenger's seat, as she drove back to Georgia. She couldn't believe that she was the same bouncy, bubbly girl that had been one of her closest friends. Her fat booty and softball size titties had whittled away to nothing. The drugs had also added forty years to her features and turned her skin several shades darker. She had an odor of death emanating from her that made Cameisha roll down her window.

"Where are we?" Dasia asked when the blast of air woke her from her slumber.

"Tennessee," she replied then countered with a question of her own. One that had been eating at her the whole ride. "What happened? How you turn into a drug addict?"

"Gurl, I been a drug addict since I was twelve years old. I was booked after I took my first puff of weed. I seen my moms smoking weed err day and couldn't wait to try it myself. Funny thing is, she the one who gave it to me. After that, boys would let me smoke so they could feel me up. Next thing you know, I'm fucking. I ain't mean to be no hoe. Niggas would tell me I was pretty and that they wanted to be my man. They would give me weed and beer, and then, after I gave them some pussy, they'd be gone! Then the next man would come with more weed, more dick and more letdown. So, I tried coke, and liked it. Then it was weed, beer, coke and dick that I was addicted to. Lisa came along and treated me good. She didn't leave me. She...she... Shit, she used me, too!"

Cameisha felt Dasia's pain as she recalled a lifetime of being used and abused herself. Her heart breaking sobs almost caused her to break-down again. She was grateful when her phone began buzzing once again from the backseat. The car swerved as she reached back to grab it.

"Hello," she answered casually.

"Hello! Are you serious? You all over the news and you saying hello!" Jackie fumed. "Where are you? Why you ain't been answering your phone?"

"Chill, ma! Err thing good. Well, it's about to be once I blaze Juan's ass at his mama's funeral."

"Girl, that's suicide!" Jackie shot back. She quickly caught on that that's what she intended. "What about Trigga?"

"Guess I'll see him when I get there," she shrugged.

"Where? ICU?" she shot back. She had no idea that she hadn't gotten the news of Trigga's survival.

"Huh? ICU? He's...alive?" she stammered in confusion.

"Girl, Samantha been calling and texting your ass for hours! Yeah, he alive! And Aqua had a boy... Hello? You still there?"

"Uh...yeah, I'm um...here," Meisha stammered as she processed the news. It changed everything. She now had a reason to live. "I still gotta do what I gotta do. I love you, Jackie."

"What... Hello? Hello!" Jackie shouted. She didn't like what she'd heard in her friend's voice. She called back, but the now powered down phone went straight to voicemail.

"What?" Dasia asked, trying to get the whole story from the half of the conversation that she'd heard.

"You wanna make things right? Take one for the team?" she replied.

"Hell yeah! Whatever you need me to do," she replied eagerly. It didn't take a rocket scientist to know that she wanted her to kill someone. She had no problem with it, no problem at all.

****

"Huh?" Big Sean asked of the modification Cameisha asked of him. He understood it perfectly and could easily do it. What had him confused was Dasia's appearance. He remembered how pretty and fine she'd been when she first arrived in town. If she hadn't been so young he would've hit that himself.

"A remote trigger," Cameisha repeated. "Like a cell phone or a..."

"Yeah, yeah, I can do it," he said in relief. Had the girl blown herself up, he would've had to deal with her uncle.

"I'm still wearing it. I just don't want to hit the switch. You go to hell if you kill yourself," she repeated. Dasia slowly nodded along in agreement. The withdrawals were getting stronger and she fought not to throw up on his pretty furniture.

Big Sean made the modifications to the suicide vest while Cameisha watched over him. It still had the handheld trigger as a fail-safe, but the primary trigger was hooked to a cell phone.

"Just press send and it's a wrap. You sure you wanna do this?" he pleaded.

"I don't have a choice," she replied. She had to stand on her tiptoes to reach his cheek, so she did so and planted a kiss there.

Big Sean reeled from the cold feel of her lips. He looked down and saw nothing but death in her eyes. The moment was shattered when Dasia threw up all over his coffee table.

****

"Feel better?" Cameisha asked as Dasia injected herself with heroin. It was diluted with water so she wouldn't go into a nod but still strong enough to her off sick, yet not strong enough to get her high since she was about to meet her maker.

"Much," she replied, shaking her head. Even she realized that it was a damn shame for a person to need anything to make them feel good. Not drugs, not a man nor any material items should be needed for that. Just thinking about the glory and greatness of God should be enough to lift anyone's spirits. God weighed heavily on her mind; knowing that she was on her way to meet Him. She wasn't the only one, though.

"Good, let's get you dressed. The funeral is about to start," Cameisha said. She had to use a bunch of safety pins to hold her dress up on Dasia's emaciated body. They'd once worn the same size until she got on the Jenny crack diet. Add that with heroin calisthenics and there was nothing left.

"My feet lost weight, too!" Dasia cracked as her foot flopped in Meisha's pumps.

"That's not funny!" Cameisha demanded but laughed anyway. She helped put a wig on her matted hair and then big shades on her eyes to cover her pockmarked face. Last but not least, the explosive laden pink mink coat from one of the stash houses.

"This is so nice," Dasia sang as she stroked the soft fur.

"You can keep it," Meisha replied dryly, cracking them both up.

The mood then turned somber again once they reached the car. They rode in total silence towards the graveyard. Only one would be returning.

****

"Fuck the police! I want her dead! If the cops catch her before you kill her, then you're dead! Do you understand me?" Juan growled from in front of his mother's casket.

His men nodded their heads in understanding. They had just witnessed him hack the body of El Capitan into bite-sized pieces and feed them to his dogs. What was left went into a dumpster. Life in prison would be better than death at his hands.

"We'll find her," Manny assured him. He wasn't quite sure if his brother's threat extended to him, too, and didn't want to find out. No sooner had the words left his mouth than he saw the familiar pink mink swaying in their direction.

The police spotted her as well.

"That bitch has balls!" Detective Walton exclaimed with an air of admiration in his voice. Marisol's murder had been captured on tape and now here was her killer at her funeral. "Huge, gorilla, King Kong sized balls!"

"Go kill her! Right now, on the spot!" Manny ordered, pushing a worker forward. He'd been wanting to fuck the man's pretty little girlfriend anyway, so the public murder would kill two birds with one stone.

"Here? Now?" the man shrieked. There were police everywhere and there was no way of escape. It was a kill or be killed order, so either way, he was doomed.

"Wait!" Juan ordered when he realized that she was headed straight towards them. Even he had to admit that she had balls to be there. "Wait 'til she gets here. I wanna see the look in her eyes when she dies!"

Cameisha pulled up the number to the bomb and placed her finger on the send button. She watched, through binoculars, as she waited for Dasia to reach the casket.

Juan smiled when who he thought was Cameisha arrived and lifted her shades. He frowned when he realized that it was Dasia instead. He opened his mouth to speak as he saw the detonator in her hand. His brain gave the command to run but it was too late.

"Adios, mi hermano," Cameisha muttered and pressed the button. She knew it was a bomb but was still shocked by the explosion.

The twenty pounds of semtex growled and grumbled for a millisecond before erupting. The deafening blast shook the ground as it vaporized Juan, Manny, Dasia and everyone else who stood within a ten-foot range. Nuts and bolts spread out at a thousand feet per second, killing and injuring even more.

"Damn!" Meisha exclaimed as a blast of the hot shock wave reached her. A nail from the bomb went clear through the car, just narrowly missing her.

"What...in...the hell...was that?" one of the cops asked as they picked themselves back up.

"That was the most gangsta shit I've ever seen in my life," Walton exclaimed. He couldn't help but clap his hands in appreciation. That should have been the end of the Dope Girl, but it wasn't.

Instead, it was just like her father had said. *"That's the thing about hustling, it's an addiction. Once you start, you can never really stop. Take breaks, maybe. Try something legit, maybe, but you'll always be back."*

Chapter 3

"In breaking news, an explosion rocked Southside Cemetery today. Police are describing the blast as a suicide attack carried out by wanted fugitive Cameisha Forrest. Forrest was wanted for the murder of veteran police officer Toshiba Watkins, along with another unnamed man. Hours after committing those murders, she was caught on tape killing Marisol Salazar, the reputed queen of The Salazar Drug Cartel. Then, in an act described by an unnamed officer as 'the most gangsta beep he'd ever seen', she detonated a suicide vest at her funeral, killing dozens more. Police are investigating rumors of her being an Islamic extremist who had pledged her allegiance to ISIS."

"Oh, here we go with the ISIS shit again! What the fuck is an Islamic extremist?" Jackie's boyfriend ranted. "Islam means peace or submission, so an Islamic extremist would be someone extremely peaceful! And how come religion only comes into play when it's Islam? When that asshole shot up a movie theatre, no one called him a Christian extremist! There is no such thing as 'Radical Islam'. Once it's been changed, it's no longer Islam! You can't do shit prohibited in Islam and still call it Islam!"

He was right but Jackie missed it all. The news of her friend's death totally took her breath away. Had she not been a beautiful shade of dark brown, she would have been blue from the lack of oxygen. It was only when she got lightheaded that she realized that she wasn't breathing. "Oh, Meisha," she moaned with her first breath. Along with it came the first tear, quickly followed by many, many more.

****

"The fuck!" Little Self demanded as he watched the news report. He choked on his blunt when Cameisha's name was mentioned. Tears from choking hid the ones from the pain of losing his big sister. She was the only family he had.

"I'm here, baby," Angel cooed and reminded him that she, too, was his family. So was their child, who was taking shape inside of her young body. She wrapped him up in her arms and rocked him gently.

That's how Bad Ass found them when he walked in. "Sucka for love ass nigga," he chuckled. "What, you so in love it just makes you weep? Keith Sweat ass nigga..."

"Meisha dead, yo," Self replied to cut off the comedy. He was used to the jokes but now wasn't the time.

Bad Ass was a confirmed bachelor. Music, movies and the media promoted licentiousness and he was all for it. 'Fuck a bitch, then fuck the bitch' was his mantra. "Say word! Yo, say word!" Bad Ass demanded. He didn't know how to cry so he just got mad. Just like Self, she was the only family he ever had. Cameisha was the only person to ever tell him that she loved him. That was perhaps the only thing that kept him from becoming a total monster. Now, she was gone.

****

"Yeah right," Aqua said as she also twisted her lips into a 'yeah right' fashion. She didn't believe a word of the news report. She knew Cameisha too well, so she knew good and damn well that she wouldn't and didn't blow herself up. Had they said she got killed when she showed up at the funeral and shot the place up, she would have believed that.

Samantha, who was in the hospital room visiting her and the baby at the time, sank slowly into a chair in stunned silence. It was crazy to her how quick, hard and far everything had changed. Just a month ago, they were raking in the dough, shopping, eating and clubbing like rock stars. "I guess I better go tell Trigga," Samantha finally spoke. He was still unconscious but she still wanted him to hear it from family.

"Well, leave my baby here," Aqua said, reaching her chubby arms out for her chubby son.

Samantha frowned at her odd reaction then shook it off. Aqua was an odd girl so why wouldn't she have an odd reaction? She figured she was trying to be strong and would get a good cry once she left. She returned the healthy baby boy to his mother and went up to the ICU.

Samantha was surprised to see the police guard had left from in front of Trigga's door. He hadn't committed a crime but the authorities knew he was linked to the cop killing Cameisha Forrest. Now that she was dead, they retired the detail. They had been ordered not to let anyone other than immediate family inside. Samantha insisted he was her brother, despite his being brown and her being white. She did have some big titties and big titties opened doors. The cops had ignored her pregnant belly in hopes of getting some head.

"Sup, buddy?" Samantha asked softly after she entered the room. Trigga didn't reply since comatose people don't often speak. She went over and held his hand as she continued to speak. "Sorry to be the bearer of bad news, but...well...I guess I may as well just say it 'cuz sometimes people try to talk around bad news to soften the blow, but to me, the anticipation just makes it worse. I would rather they just came right out and say what they're gonna say and get it over with. Cameisha is dead! She took her enemies with her but she's gone. Now Mister, you have two choices. You can go be with her and Troy or stay here with me. Well, not with me, with me. I mean, with me. With us, me, Aqua and little Stevie. Oh, and Self and that bad ass little Bad Ass. We're family."

"Chile, you gonna talk that po' boy to death!" Nurse Brown fussed when she came in. His blood pressure was noticeably higher so she shooed Samantha from the room. When she turned back to the patient, a tear ran down his handsome face. His hand moved so she called for the doctor.

****

Trigga blinked rapidly, trying to make the lights come on but they didn't. His ears worked just fine and he didn't like what he'd heard one bit. Most of the technical jargon went a mile or so over his head but words like 'blind' and 'permanent' he understood.

"Once the swelling goes down, he should be just fine," the doctor said, puffing out his chest. Silly rabbit still thought it was his skillset that saved the patient. Little did he know, he could die from a splinter if God willed it.

"It's a miracle! Nothing short of a miracle!" Nurse Brown exclaimed. She clasped her hands and raised her head to send thanks where they belonged. By the time she opened her eyes again, it was just her and the patient.

"Guess I ain't never gone see nothing again, huh?" Trigga croaked. He pretty much surmised that much but wanted to hear it.

"Dead people don't see, talk, eat or nothing else! So be thankful for yo' life, chile! You got shot in yo' head!"

"You're right. I'm is...I mean, I am," he corrected. "I don't even 'member getting shot. Last thing I member was talking to my girl, then, I woke up here?"

"Well, that was a couple days ago. Yo little white girlfriend come by err day. She claim she yo sister."

"White? That must be Samantha. Guess you could say she is my sister," Trigga replied after a moment's thought.

On cue, Samantha ambled in for her daily visit. "Hey there Mister Man! I heard you were awake!" she cheered so cheerfully that Trigga pictured her in a cheerleader's outfit with pom-poms.

"Yeah, I ain't too long woke up. What happened to me? Where's Meisha?"

"Oh boy," Samantha said sadly as she sank into a chair. She took a deep breath and told him what she knew in one long run-on sentence. It concluded with, "Cameisha is gone. Her funeral is in a few days."

"Funeral?" He wondered what was left to be buried after an explosion like that. No DNA test were done on the remains since the police stated it was Cameisha. The medical examiner just gave whatever family member that came by a bag of flesh or bones to bury. At least they had something to put in a casket.

"Okay, that's enough. This man needs some rest. He got shot in his head, you know," Nurse Brown huffed as she shooed her out the room once more.

"Okay. I'll see you tomorrow. Aqua took her son home, so I guess I'll go bug them," she said. She blew her big brother a kiss from the doorway then turned to leave. She didn't see the nurse swat the kiss away before it could reach him.

Chapter 4

Cameisha watched Samantha leave the condo and head to her car. Her round belly brought a smile to her face. Seeing her mouth move a mile a minute as she spoke to herself made her chuckle and shake her head. She loved Samantha dearly but knew the girl couldn't hold water. It was her loose lips that had sunk their ship. Never mind the fact that Samantha had no idea that Cameisha had kept Juan in the dark about the altered drugs. Cameisha was too selfish to accept to blame. However, she was wise enough to keep her secret from the talkative girl.

"I know you ain't went to get twenty turkey burgers that quick!" Aqua called out when she heard the front door open. Samantha had just left on her mission so no way she could've made it there and back in five minutes.

"What, no more Fat-Fat Burgers?" Cameisha quipped as she eased into the room. She'd expected Aqua to jump up, rush across the room and put her in an Aqua hug. An Aqua hug packed a little more pressure than a bear hug but not quite as much as a Grandma Deidre hug. Instead, she got...

"Oh, hey, Cameisha. I been waiting on you," Aqua said while little Stevie dined on breast milk.

"'Hey, Cameisha'? That's all? I'm back from the dead and all I get is, 'hey, Cameisha'?" she asked, feeling a little hurt by the lukewarm reception.

"Girl, please! I knew you wasn't dead! I'm not slow, you know!"

"Who else knows?" she asked urgently. Her survival depended upon her being thought dead. She needed help and only trusted Aqua for the job. Jackie was solid as a rock but had a man. Chicks sometimes told their men their secrets. Had she used Samantha, it would have gone viral in minutes.

"No one that I know of. You know I can keep a secret!" Aqua said in a tone that proved it. "You talked to Trigga? He woke up."

"No. I have to leave everything and everyone...including him. I love Trigga, but I'm on the run."

"Aww, man!" Aqua mourned the loss of their relationship. "At least meet your nephew Stevie."

"Hey, little man," Auntie Meisha cooed as she picked up the heavy baby. Tears began to seep when she thought about not being around to watch him grow up. Not having children of her own to play with him.

Aqua let her weep until she finished and gave her the baby back. "So, now what?" she asked.

"I got some stuff I gotta get out of my condo. I don't know if the police are still there or not. I doubt it since I'm dead, but I can't take that chance. I can't take any chances."

"You know I got you," Aqua said like Cameisha knew that she would.

"Good," she said. Cameisha grabbed a pillow and comforter and walked into the walk-in closet. She made a pallet and fell asleep two seconds after laying down.

****

"Good morning, mister man," Nurse Brown sang as she breezed into the room. "Time for your sponge bath."

The job was usually handled by one of the CNAs while he was asleep, but the nurse overheard the ratchet nurse's assistant talking about his dick to another one. She decided to take over the task to preserve his dignity, and yeah, she wouldn't mind seeing some dick.

"Cain't I just get into the shower?" he complained. Trigga was quite the dick slinger but felt shy in front of the sweet woman. He didn't know how old she was but her mature speech gave a hint that she was old enough to be his aunt, if not his mom.

"First of all, you can't walk. After a head trauma like you suffered, you gotta learn to do stuff all over again. You'll be transferred to a rehabilitation center in a few days," she explained. "And second of all, NO!"

Trigga let out a helpless sigh as she began to wash his feet and legs. The warm, sudsy water felt good on his skin. The soft touch and sweet smell of a woman with it had him fighting not to get an erection as she worked her way up his leg. A penis has a head, with no brain, but a mind of its own.

"Really?" Nurse Brown asked, shaking her head when she reached his rock hard erection. She couldn't help but marvel at it as it throbbed and jumped.

"My bad," he said sheepishly. The nurse sighed and began to wash it. "Sss!"

"Poor baby," she pouted at his reaction to being touched. She looked around before wrapping her hand around it. Using the soapy water as a lubricant, she began to stroke it. It didn't take long before he climaxed, sending semen high into the air.

"Shit! Whew...I'm sorry," Trigga managed to get out.

"Don't be," the nurse said as she continued to pull on his erection. The first one was for him but this one was for her. She wished she could hop on and take it for a ride. Instead, she stroked, twisted and pulled it until he came again. She then laid his dick on his stomach and finished his bath.

"Nurse Brown," Trigga called as she prepared to leave the room. "How old are you?"

"Twenty-two," she replied, subtracting thirty-years.

He couldn't see the sly smile on her face or the extra sway in her hips as she left the room.

****

"Come on, she gone," Aqua whispered to Cameisha in the closet.

"If she gone, then why you whispering?" Cameisha whispered back.

"I'on know," she replied, still whispering. They both cracked up as Cameisha came out of the closet.

Samantha had left for her daily activities, allowing Cameisha to stay dead. Aqua fixed a diaper bag while Cameisha watched proudly. They made it down to the car and began the drive across town.

"I really appreciate this," Cameisha said as she drove. She couldn't help but notice the disturbed look upon Aqua's face when she spoke to her. "What? What's wrong?"

"Your breath! I'ma find your toothbrush while I'm in there, too! That's more important than some lil' books," Aqua reeled indignantly.

"What? No, you didn't!" she exclaimed. Cameisha huffed her breath into her hand to smell it for herself. "It's in the master bath! The pink one!"

Cameisha parked at the second closest train station from her condo building. Aqua left the diaper bag along with her baby with Cameisha and boarded the train. When she arrived at the next stop, she pulled out her phone and called Cameisha.

"How's my baby?" she wanted to know first and foremost.

"The same as he was when you left him...four minutes ago! Sleep. Now how it look over there?" Meisha shot back.

"Oh, okay. Well, I don't see no cops," she replied. Being from the Bronx, she knew how to spot an undercover cop from a mile away. She casually strode into the building like she belonged. "I'm in the elevator now."

"Okay, switch to video," she said and hung up. A few seconds later, the phone beeped, indicating a video call. It was now like she was there in the unit with Aqua as she entered. "Okay, in the bedroom, go in...the bedroom! Where are you going?"

"To find your toothbrush!" Aqua answered defiantly. Meisha shook her head as her friend checked the hall bathroom and then the master.

"The pink one," she reminded her when she saw her granite counters came into view. Something else on the counter caught her eye. "What's that? Right there!"

"It's a..." Aqua said as she checked. "A pregnancy test. Somebody pregnant."

Cameisha could actually hear all the air being sucked from her body. She suddenly remembered taking the test but Trigga had rushed her out before it finished processing. They'd rushed out to make it to the drug deal where Trigga had been shot. She ended up having to leave a half-of-a-million dollars behind in the car.

"Um...hello?" Aqua said, pointing the camera at her face. Five whole minutes had passed since the discovery of the test strip. The discovery of the test strip. The discovery that she was with child. Trigga, who she had to leave behind, his child.

"Um...yeah...my bad. Okay, check inside my top drawer, with the panties in it."

"This the top drawer," Aqua said, aiming the phone inside.

"Okay, now reach to the top of the drawer. Feel the pouch up there?"

"Yeah, I got it!" she cheered and came out with the bank books.

"That's it! Come on! Wait! Grab the Prada shoe box in the closet." She remembered that it was stuffed with the cash she'd needed to disappear. "Oh, and the pregnancy test!"

Chapter 5

"I'm ready for my next bath," Trigga announced when he heard soft the sound of soft nurse's shoes enter his room.

"Why, you peed the bed?" came the reply that made him sit straight up in bed.

His sightless eyes went wide from shock. "Cameisha? Oh shit, I'm dead! Aww, man, I done died," he griped and fell back. He knew Cameisha was dead, so for him to hear her, that clearly meant that he must have died, too.

"I sure hope you're on morphine, codeine or something! Anything but beats being that damn dumb," she laughed as she went over to him.

"They said you were dead!" he sobbed as they embraced.

"Nope, but they are! Juan, his mama and the nigga who shot you!" she replied.

"Yo, Meish, you must be hot as fuck! They say you killed a cop!"

"I did. That's why I gotta stay dead. I'm leaving. Going with my grandma n'dem. You staying here or coming with?"

"Say no more!" he said and swung his legs off the bed. He hoisted himself up with a grunt...and fell flat on his face. "Can I get a lil' help?"

"Wait there," she said, as if he had a choice. She rushed out and returned with a wheelchair. It took some doing to get him into it since neither knew to lock the wheels. Once he was in, she rushed from the room.

"Be easy, shawty," Trigga said when he felt how fast she was pushing him. He couldn't see but was sure it would look suspect.

"You right," she agreed and slowed down. "I would hate to have to shoot up a damn hospital."

She didn't have to shoot up the hospital since they made it safely outside. Trigga used his arms to pull up while she pushed to get him inside the vehicle. Cameisha knew where she was going although the how was still a mystery. She knew it wasn't as simple as driving to the airport and boarding a flight. That would require IDs and passports. Both of which would get her the death penalty.

"Where we headed?" Trigga asked, not knowing if they were driving north, south, east or west.

"West. I figure we can get to Mexico and then fly to South America," she replied, hoping it would be as easy as it sounded.

"If we can get to Belize, maybe Rude Boy can help us," he suggested.

Cameisha mulled it over for a few seconds before nodding her head in agreement. "Knew you were good for something besides making babies," she shot back with a smile Trigga could hear through his darkness.

"For real? You serious?" he asked through a smile of his own. He would never know it was the only reason she didn't leave without him.

****

"This will have to do," Cameisha said of the rundown motel she pulled into just as they crossed into Louisiana She was dead tired by the time they'd reached Mississippi but had refused to stop in the state. She practically held her breath the whole way through while fighting to maintain the speed limit.

Trigga moved his head back and forth as if looking around. He couldn't see but heard the hustle and bustle of a trap motel. The pitter patter of dope boys and the opening and closing of car doors as prostitutes turned tricks. He nodded in agreement since he knew the faces on money were the only IDs needed to rent a room here. He listened to the familiar sounds as she went to get them a room.

"Shit! Fucking shit!" Meisha fussed as she struggled to get the stolen wheelchair out of the trunk. It took her twice as long to open it as it did to close it, but she finally got it.

"You gotta lock the wheels," an addict said, seeing the couple struggling. She came over and demonstrated how to do it.

"Thank you," Meisha said with a twenty-dollar tip.

"No, thank you!" she cheered at the equivalent of two sucked dicks. She held the bill up like it was the Olympic torch and rushed to give it to one of the dope boys.

"Eww," Cameisha said when the motel's funk kicked her in her nose. An air sample would show a mix of blood, sweet, tears, cum, menthol, malt liquor, piss, shit, crack, weed and nail polish remover.

"Smell like money," Trigga laughed. He'd made a small fortune hustling in and around rooms that smelled just like this one.

"Man, as much as I hate to, I gotta lay on this bed," she whined. It was nasty, but she was dead tired so had no choice. She helped Trigga on and then climbed on top of him. Any thoughts of getting some were dashed when she began snoring seconds later.

"Goodnight, sweetheart."

****

"Mmm," Cameisha moaned when she awoke on top of her man. She could feel his morning erection throbbing beneath her. "Fuck this!"

"I know that's right!" Trigga laughed as she struggled to get his dick out. She only pulled one leg out of her pants and panties before lowering her soaked vagina on his dick.

"Mmm," she moaned again and winced from the pain filled pleasure and sank slowly down. It only took two rocks of her hips for her to get her rocks off. Once she recovered from the badly needed orgasm, she rocked him to one as well.

"Shit!" he howled as she squeezed his pulsating dick inside of her. She waited until she felt it deflate before getting up.

"Mm...mm," she said, shaking her head from side to side as she came out of the bathroom. She would rather ride all day full of cum than get into that shower.

It was just after 9am when they got back on the road. Mexico was still days away so there was no time to waste.

She was still driving when her funeral was held back in Atlanta.

****

"I can't!" Jackie moaned and fell back on her bed. This was her third attempt at putting on the black dress, but she just couldn't do it. "I'm not going!"

"You have to," Ralphie assured her.

She'd made it as far as her panties, bra and black hose before he had to assist her with the dress. He lifted her, rolled her and zipped her up. He gave her foot a peck before slipping the black pumps on. He half-carried her out to the car since her legs couldn't support both her weight and her grief. Cameisha being dead was one thing but putting her in the ground was a whole different story.

Aqua was the only person calm enough to handle the arrangements. She'd picked out the picture that would be blown up to be placed beside the closed casket. It wasn't one of the fly girl glamour shots of recent. Instead, she chose one from being happy.

It was Aqua who'd called Dasia's mother and relayed the bad news. Saleria didn't seemed shocked since she knew her daughter's chosen lifestyle didn't come with a long life. It had only been a matter of when her bad habits and poor choices would claim her. Saleria didn't have the money to fly down so Aqua sprang for the tickets for her and Dasia's son.

"What?" Aqua asked when she saw the skeptical look Samantha gave her.

Her lips were twisted and her head cocked like 'what you got going on?' "You're two calm. You were closer to her than all of us, yet you haven't shed a tear. Not a one!" Samantha said.

Aqua just shrugged and kept doing what she was doing.

****

"Somebody gone pay for this!" Bad Ass growled. He'd turned his grief into anger and was ready to murder something.

"Who? She took 'em all with her," Self said with a slight chuckle. The shit was so gangster that it made him proud.

"Took them with her," Angel repeated softly. They were the same words but with different meaning. She knew that suicide was a ticket to hell and could only assume the bad men who went with her were in the fire as well.

Angel loved bad boys, but knew what went with it. Self was a bad boy so she wondered which would claim him. Would she and their child have to visit him in prison or the grave? She made up her mind at that moment to steer him away from the streets. She knew that meant keeping him away from Bad Ass.

"Well, I'ma bust any Mexican I see," Bad Ass vowed.

Angel nodded her head at her decision to come between them.

"Would Meisha want us to do that?" Self asked, already knowing the answer.

"Guess not. But, let them niggas on Glenwood come short! I'ma air that shit out!"

Little Self stayed mute despite Cameisha's advice just to cut them off if they came short. They had work out in the streets and needed every cent so that they could secure a new connect. Self and Bad Ass were dope boys and dope boys sell dope.

****

"Ca-me, Camisol, Ca-meesha was a sweet girl. An angel plucked from the Earth to go back to heaven where she belonged!" the rented preacher preached.

The man had never met her a day in his life so he freestyled the eulogy. She did look angelic in the picture so he went with it. His mouth was dry form the weed he'd smoked on the way to the gravesite so he sipped water between lies. Cameisha was no angel, she was a dope girl. A dope girl and a killer who only cared about herself.

Jackie's wails and moans drowned out half of what he was saying. She was absolutely inconsolable and it spread to Samantha. The usually talkative girl missed the sermon due to her own sobbing. Besides, they knew her. The good, the bad and the ugly.

"Your mom is in there," Saleria told her grandson. The child looked confused as he processed the information. He clearly recognized Cameisha's face since she used to come by their apartment. Dasia had treated him more like a little brother than a son.

Saleria bowed and asked for forgiveness for her daughter's sins. She crossed herself, then kissed her crucifix, hoping it would benefit the girl. She did want to do some sightseeing and hit a club later, so she turned to leave.

"You take care of yourself, Aqua!" she said in a motherly tone. "Thank you for being her friend."

"I should be thanking her," Aqua replied. They shared a hug and she was off.

All eyes gravitated to the handsome stranger on the perimeter of the service. His eyes couldn't be seen behind his dark shades that matched his dark suit and dark demeanor. He had a loud presence without speaking a word.

"Who was that woman?" Jackie asked once Dasia/Cameisha was lowered into the ground.

"Saleria," Aqua replied as if she would know who she was. Jackie didn't come from their projects, so had no clue as to who that was. Aqua saw the unanswered question still on her face and explained, "Dasia's mom with her son."

"Dasia's mom? Why would she be here?" Jackie wondered. She couldn't fathom why Cameisha's own beloved grandmother wasn't there. She knew she was in South America but just knew that she'd come for her funeral. Jackie was a smart girl and figured it all out. "Un uh! No way!"

"Way!" was all Aqua replied. "But she can't know!"

"Oh hell no!" she said, following Dasia's eyes to Samantha. Sam was their sister but she was their talk too damned much sister. Their sister who couldn't hold water. Her eyes then went back to the stranger behind the shades. "So, who is that?"

"I'on know," Aqua shrugged.

The crew all departed and headed home to live their lives. Once the place was deserted, the man moved forward.

"Bravo," Cameron Forrest clapped. He'd heard from his grandmother Diedra about the ruse. Still, he had to show up to admire his daughter's handiwork. "Good job. I see you learned well. Good thing, too, 'cuz I'm coming back for my city."

Chapter 6

After a long bus ride through Mexico, Cameisha and Trigga reached the border of Belize. He had plenty movement in his legs but still couldn't walk on his own. It took a two hundred dollar bribe to get the passport-less couple through Immigration. Another bus delivered them to the city of Belize several hours later. A call to Rude Boy had him standing out front when they arrived in a taxi.

"First time mi see a ghost!" Rude Boy cheered when Cameisha stepped from the cab. He saw her struggling with Trigga and rushed to help. "Leave him to me."

"Thank you," she said wearily. They'd had to ditch the wheelchair in Mexico City. Since then, she'd had to practically carry him.

"Sup, shawty?" Trigga said, sounding vulnerable. Losing his sight was bad enough but having to be carried by your pregnant girlfriend added insult to injury.

"Chillin', Big Dog. Let's get you guys to a room," he said and help them. "No luggage?"

"Nah. We ain't on vacation this time," Meisha replied. Besides the twenty thousand left in the money belt under her shirt, they had nothing.

"Rosa! Rosa! Rosa!" Rude Boy yelled. On cue, the cute waitress named Rosa popped up. "Run and grab them a few things."

"Okay," she said, accepting the fistful of dollars. She turned and looked the couple up and down before deciding, "Size 7 and...extra-large?"

"She's good!" Meisha said in admiration. The girl had worked as a seamstress in Guatemala before migrating north. She'd been headed for America but Rude Boy got her first. Now that she had a man and a job, she'd forgotten all about America.

****

"Whew!" Cameisha said as she removed her crusty panties. She balled them up, intending to throw them away instead of trying to wash them. Rosa had picked up underclothes as well as outfits for both of them. After a meal, they'd finally got the chance to bathe and rest.

"Don't use all the hot water!" Trigga called from the bedroom.

"Ha-ha!" she called back. The quaint hotel didn't actually have hot water but the water was warm from the sun on the roof top tank. Cameisha was thankful for the name brand douche in the bag. The long ride left her feeling dirty both inside and out so she cleaned herself both inside and out.

Once she washed away the three days' worth of dirt, she set a chair in the shower. She then helped Trigga inside and left him to wash himself. She knew him well enough to know his dignity was hurting. She laid out on one of the twin beds and looked up at the ceiling.

"Hey! This is the room!" she popped up and shouted.

"What room?" Trigga asked from the bathroom.

She ran inside the bathroom to answer. "From the first time we came! The first time we made love!" she replied.

"Shole is," he said, looking around but not seeing anything.

"You so stupid!" she huffed and went back into the room. A wicked smile spread across her face as she contemplated some get back.

"I'm done. Can you come help me?" Trigga called. He stroked himself semi-erect to put on a good show.

"Sure, I..." she sang sweetly, but got stuck on the dick.

He smiled a smug little smile at her dilemma. Come to find out, the joke was about to be on him.

"Here you go," Meisha was still singing when she delivered him to one of the beds. To his surprise, she got on the other. He just knew his hard dick snare had lured her in. "What you doing?"

"Going to bed," she replied as if it were a silly question. "I'm about to...mmm...play in this...mmm...good...sss...pussy first, though."

Trigga was totally confused by her answer. To make matters worse, he could clearly hear her vagina getting wetter and wetter as she played in it. It was soon squishing in harmony with her soft whimpers and moans. He got so hard so quick, he might have gone blind if he wasn't already.

"Let me get some of that, shawty!" he pleaded.

"Come...sss...and...mmm...get some," she dared. It started out as a joke to tease him but nothing was funny about how hard she came.

"Damn!" Trigga exclaimed, hearing all the commotion coming from the next bed. Meisha thrashed around almost violently form busting a nut. That didn't stop her, though, and the greedy girl went for seconds. "You know I can't walk."

"Too bad cuz this shit is so hot it's burning my fingers!" she teased him and her swollen clit at the same. "Mmm...sss...mmm!"

"Fuck this!" Trigga declared and hoisted himself up. He stood and wobbled like a baby standing for the first time. He had to extend his arms to keep his balance.

"That's right, baby! Come get some of this good pussy!" she urged as he took his first step.

A few steps later, he fell face first on her bed. Good thing her vagina was there to break his fall. He clamped his lips on her lips and sucked them like one of the sweet mangos the country was famous for.

"Shit!"

"Mm-hm," Trigga agreed as she came once more. He then scrambled up to let her taste her own juices off his lips and face. He used the opportunity to shove his throbbing erection inside of her.

"Shit!" she grunted as he filled her up. She knew a pounding was coming for being a tease. She grabbed handfuls of the sheets to brace herself.

He gave it to her just like she expected. Unexpectedly, he pushed her legs up and got on his knees. They were both spent and winded by their third mutual climax.

"Guess what...shawty," Trigga said, trying to catch his breath.

"What, bae?" she asked.

"I can walk!"

****

"Whoa, look who's walking! It's a miracle!" Rude Boy clapped when a wobbly Trigga wobbled into the dining area.

"Yeah, something like that," he replied. Cameisha wore a crooked, cocky smile, knowing it was that good pussy that made him walk.

"So, what's the plan? You guys staying awhile?" the owner asked. Trigga didn't know the answer so he turned to where he knew Meisha was standing.

"Yeah, we need to lay low for a second," she replied. She needed Trigga to be a hundred percent for the rest of their trip. They were safe here and knew that Rude Boy could be trusted. "We're going to need travel docs."

"No problem. Ten bands should get it," he nodded. It would be enough to bribe someone in Immigration out of a pair of passports. That would allow the couple to fly the rest of the way to Brazil instead of another perilous bus journey.

"Sounds good. We need some breakfast so he can go through his next round of therapy," she said, causing Trigga to smile.

He was about to get some more of that vibrant vagina.

Chapter 7

"Look," Flip chuckled when he saw Self's car pull into their apartment complex on Glenwood.

"He dead!" Flop laughed. They both knew he was there for the fifty grand they owed for the dope he'd fronted them. They also knew that Cameisha was the man and that she was dead. That's why they'd tricked off half of the money and had zero plans on giving him the rest.

"Sup, yo," Self asked as he hopped out. He extended his hand to give them both a pound like they'd done when things were all good. They refused eyed contact with the pound which meant it was all bad. It was about to get worse, though.

"Err thang a lil slow, shawty. We ain't got that up yet. Holla later," Flop said, looking away as he spoke.

"Yeah, later," Flip seconded, nodding in agreement.

Self nodded, too, as he scoped out their new jeans, sneaker and jewels. "A'ight. I got something to do later, so my nigga Bad Ass gon' fall through, later," Little Self said. He flipped his NY fitted cap to the back and got back into his car. "Later!"

"Yeah, my nigga, later!" Flip laughed. Him and Flop shared a pound and a laugh.

It was short lived because the hat adjustment was a signal. Later came sooner than either expected.

Bad Ass whipped up into the parking lot with Devin riding shotgun with a pump shotgun. The passenger began dumping before Bad Ass could even come to a complete stop. The buckshot made Flop do a full flip. Flip turned to run but Bad Ass leveled his Mac on his back. A three shot burst left him flopping on the ground like a fish out of water. They had a point to prove so they pointed their guns at everyone outside to prove it. Once they finished shooting, two more lay dead and five more were wounded. Several of those shot were bystanders but only one was innocent.

"My baby! My baby! They done shot my baby!" a young mother wailed over her dead child.

"We out!" Bad Ass shouted and jumped back into the car. Devin came behind him and they chirped off.

****

"Well, what now?" Self asked out loud. He was primarily talking to Cameisha, trying to figure out what she would advise.

"Shit, we still got what...sixty bands? We can shoot up top and cop a few bricks. At least three?" Bad Ass replied.

"We can definitely get at least three. My cousin Rich will hook us up," Self agreed. "Guess Flip and Flop can keep that."

"Hell naw! I'ma fuck they bitches and find out where they stashed that bread. I want all mine! I'm like the new Alpo out this bitch!" he exclaimed.

"Oh no!" Angel wailed from the living room. Self jumped up and rushed in to see what upset her.

"Sucka for love ass nigga," Bad Ass said and came in behind him.

"What's wrong, bae?" he asked, swooping in beside her on the sofa.

"Look!" she said, pointing at the T.V. The news was on and they were the top story.

"A three-year-old child was shot and killed today at a Decatur apartment complex. One of four people killed in what police say was a drug related shooting..."

Little Self snapped his head to his partner for a reaction. Bas Ass simply shrugged it off. Like rapper Rakim said, "The streets are no place for bystanders to stand."

"She cute," he said of the child's crying mother on the screen. "I may have to hit that too!"

Self squinted at his friend, trying to recognize him. He was turning into a monster right before his eyes. They came from a land of monsters so he knew what they looked like.

Bad Ass was indeed becoming a monster, but what did the world expect? Both his parents chose a crack pipe over 'act right' and neglected him from day one. His dad died first trying to rob a bodega. Papi behind the counter put one in his head as he fled the store. The kid had to see the man who killed his father almost every day of his life.

Mom went out bad as well. Her heart exploded right in front of him when he was ten years old. He'd lived with her corpse for a week, until the smell alerted the neighbors. The child still lived in the projects after the deaths of his parents. He slept in staircases, on rooftops and friends' sofas. Damn right he was becoming a monster.

****

"Say, shawty! You heard the news?" Devin asked anxiously when Bad Ass reached the trap. The trap stars were completely out of dope now but still hung out in the trap. A steady flow of junkies came and went and came back again, hoping to get high. If they didn't get something soon, the trap would dry up and die.

"What news?" Bad Ass frowned at his shook up demeanor. He was glad no one else was around to see it but even gladder no one was around to hear it.

"They say we killed a baby!" he said, frazzled by his conscious. The streets are no place for scruples.

"They said it got hit by buckshot, so technically, you killed a baby," he corrected. "It's all good, though. You know I ain't gonna say shit. You good, yo."

"Hell naw, I ain't good! I cain't like with that. I...I...I gotta turn myself in! My grandmamma ain't raise me like this! I...I gotta..."

"Chill the fuck out is what you gotta do! You talking crazy, B! They gone give your ass the death penalty. Shit, you may as well kill yo'self! Now here, take a puff and calm down," Bad Ass said, extending the blunt.

"I...don't...know...man," Devin said between drags on the smoldering cigar. He pulled so hard, the blunt began burning lopsided.

"Here, nigga," he barked, taking the blunt back. He used saliva to slow it down so it would burn evenly. "Nigga, that's part of the game. Shit happens, yo. You ain't mean that shit, so live with it."

"I cain't, shawty! That shit ain't right! That was just a kid, mane!" he wailed, crying tears.

Bad Ass was disgusted by what he was witnessing. This was the same dude talking real rough on the way over to Glenwood about how he was about light these niggas up and now he standing with snot coming out his nose. No way was this punk not going to give him up, too. He may as well ride over to the police station with him and save the cops some gas. May as well put a gun to his own temple and save the state a lethal injection. May as well...

"You right, yo," Bad Ass agreed. "You gotta take responsibility."

"I do? I am? I...mean, yeah. I do," Devin said. He stuck his chest out in nobility at doing the right thing.

"Hell yeah, mane! I'm proud of you! You need some dough for a lawyer? Don't go down there without no lawyer, B!" he urged.

"Nah, all my bread... I'm saying, though, nah!" he stammered. Like most dope boys, he'd fucked up all his money. Tricked it off at the mall, with the weed man and young girls.

"I got you, yo. Just don't say my name while you down there."

"Never that!" Devin proclaimed like it was true. He had no intentions on snitching, but most snitches don't. However, things change once they get into the interrogation room. Penises shrivel up and turn into vaginas as men turn pussy.

"Okay, bet. I trust you. Let's go get this dough. It's stashed next door to Misty Waters," Bad Ass said and began the short walk to the apartment complex next door. He was relieved to hear Devin behind him.

"You must got a broad over here," Devin asked as they went through a hole in the fence that separated the two properties.

"Huh? Oh, nah. I got too much cash to trust a bitch with. I got my shit stashed in the woods behind the complex."

"That's a good idea! See, that's what I shoulda done. I..." he rambled on as he followed him to the edge of the woods. "I'll wait here. Know you don't want nobody seeing the stash."

"Nigga, you my nigga! I trust you! Come on," Bad Ass announced. He led Devin into the woods searching for the right spot. "Here we go. Right there, under that rock."

"This one?" he asked, pointing where he was pointing. When Bad Ass nodded, he bent down to lift the rock.

Devin never knew what hit him when he got shot in the back of his head. He fell face down into the red Georgia clay, turning it even redder with his blood. Bad Ass fired once more to make sure he was dead. He then emptied the rest of the clip into his body because that's what monsters do.

Chapter 8

"Sup, Richie-Rich! This is Little Self," Self greeted when his cousin took his call. He felt like a big shot calling about buying a few kilos. The last time they saw each other Self was begging for a few crumbs to sell just so he could eat.

"Little Sammy?" Rich asked, to remind him of his given name.

Self hadn't heard it in so long it gave him a brief pause. "Yeah, it's me, but they call me Self now. Little Self," he explained.

"Well, Lil' Self, shit tight right now. I ain't got no extra shake at the moment. Holla when you need a brick," he said, ready to hang up.

"Aaah! That's me hollering. I need a few bricks," Self said.

"A few? Son, they eighteen five...each!" Rich laughed, but not for long.

"I'll take three! That's fifty-five five, right?" he shot back, doing the math off the top of his head.

"Yeah, okay, my nigga. You show up with the bread and I got you. Tell you what, I'll even give 'em to you for fiddy even. That way you can cap five racks for yourself."

"That's a bet! I'll be through tomorrow," he smiled and clicked off.

"It's good?" Bad Ass asked hopefully. He could tell by the smile on Self's face that it was, but he needed to hear it.

"Son, we 'bout to come up!" Self cheered. They high-fived and danced around in celebration. "Now go get ready. We leave in an hour."

Technically, they could have left right then, but Self wanted an hour to say goodbye to Angel. He rushed up the steps the second his partner left and jumped on the bed.

"Yo, I gotta shoot up top for a sec," he said, planting kisses all over her face and neck.

She knew what that meant and lifted her hips to help him get her panties off. "When you coming...mmm...back?" Angel purred. She got a little distracted when her nipple entered his mouth.

Self missed the question when he slid into her hot box. It would have to wait a few minutes until he got off. That's all it took to for him to go stiff from a climax. Angel didn't get to cum often, but pleasing him pleased her.

"I said...when...you...coming back?" she giggled and squeezed her tight vagina even tighter, causing him to squirm. It's times like this that dudes give up way too much information. Loose lips sink ships and nothing loosens lips like tight vagina lips.

"My cousin Rich up in Harlem got some work for us. We 'bout to shoot up there and grab it and bring it back. He said eighteen five, but he gonna let me..."

"Do you really think it's a good idea for two young black men to be driving thirteen hours with dope in the car?" Angel asked, making it sound exactly like the bad idea that it was.

"Well..." he replied when he heard it. They would be lucky to get past Jersey without getting pulled over. Once a K-9 got a whiff of the blow, it would be over.

"Well, pay my mama to drive y'all. She getting paid so it'll be on her if y'all do get stopped," she explained. Angel was perfectly comfortable with sacrificing her mother for her man. Why not, since the woman chose dope over her?

"That's a good idea. Get her ready while I grab a shower."

****

"Where she going, and what she got on?" Bad Ass wondered when he saw Angel's mom coming to the car with Self. They'd cleaned her up and put her church clothes on her.

"Miss Johnson gonna drive back once we get straight. Po-po won't give her a second look."

Bad Ass stood there frowning while searching for words to shoot down the idea. In the end, he couldn't find any because it was a good idea.

"A'ight. Hop yo' ass in the backseat," he conceded and put the car in gear. As soon as both doors were closed, he pulled off.

Self and Bad Ass proved Angel right by sparking a blunt once they got moving. As soon as it went out, they lit another one. By the time they reached South Carolina, they were on their third blunt. Miss Johnson patiently waited for one of them to pass it back but it never happened.

"Can I get a toke?" she finally asked when they passed the North Carolina boarder.

"Hell naw!" Bad Ass laughed. Self didn't want to laugh at his mother-in-law, but the good weed wouldn't have it any other way. He fought off a snicker before cracking up.

"Why, cuz I suck dick?" she asked with the answer. That was exactly why they didn't want to smoke with her.

"Bingo!" Bad Ass howled and kept laughing.

"So. I like weed and dick," she proclaimed as she crossed her arms and pouted.

"We need gas, yo," Self said when the low gas light came on.

"I thought we was running out of weed!" his partner joked. He put on the turn signal to merge over to the next exit. "Your turn to drive."

"A'ight," Self responded as he went inside to pay while Bad Ass pumped the gas. When he came back, Bad Ass hopped in the backseat with Miss Johnson. Self shook his head as his partner got some head.

****

"We here!" Self called into the backseat.

"Damn! Already? That was quick as hell!" Bad Ass replied.

"That's cuz you got your dick sucked the whole way! That's got to be a record!" Self said.

"Not even close!" Miss Johnson cheered. "I rode the Greyhound out to Cali one time and..."

"Hold that thought, Ma. We'll be back," Self interrupted and got out.

Bad Ass hopped out and took a deep breath of New York air. He couldn't help but notice how different it tasted. Not better or worse, just different.

Self led the way into the pissy tenement building and opted to climb the pissy steps over riding in the pissy elevator. The smell only strengthened his resolve to never live in New York again. Bad Ass had a content look on his face to be back. Georgia was a little too slow despite the fast money. He vowed to come back once he got his weight up. It was his four-year plan, sorta like college and go pro.

"Who?" Rich barked, despite peering through the peephole. It was some New York shit that out-of-towners wouldn't understand.

"Self," he called out even though he knew he saw him. More New York shit. The sound of multiple locks and dead bolts being unlocked and unbolted could be heard out in the hall.

"Little Sammy!" Rich teased with his outstretched hand.

Self twisted his lips at the slight but accepted the pound. "Self," he repeated. "You remember Bad Ass."

"Yeah, what's up, my dude! I see y'all got put on down there in GA!" Rich said. He was a wild man himself and respected the wild man-child.

"Hell yeah! We..."

"We working for a nigga down there. He put up the dough for this pack," Self cut in. Just because they were related didn't mean he trusted him. "As long as everything is good, we can come back."

"That's what's up," Rich shrugged. He could tell that there was a little more to the story but left it alone. The price of coke had dropped in the city but they could still charge out of town customers the old rate. "Keep it coming."

The thing about the streets is, everyone you deal with is a crook. A thief, a killer, an addict or all the above. No one could or should be trusted. That's why Rich counted every bill and Little Self broke the three birds down to check for pockets of cut. They both finished at about the same time.

"A'ight, cuz. We'll be back in a couple weeks if you still be on," Self said.

"Nigga, I stay on! I got a hun'ed bricks in the room right now!" he shot back. Bas Ass shot a greedy glance to the door Rich pointed at. A lick like that would sure taste sweet. Luckily, he was his man's family.

"You buggin', yo," Self admonished on the stairs.

"What?" he asked, stifling a laugh as if he didn't know what he meant.

"Nigga, you was drooling when he said he had all that work! Shit, me too! He lucky for two things. First, he fam, and second, he flexin'! That nigga just the man next to the man!"

"If you say so," Bad Ass replied dubiously. He was a shoe off and flaunted what he had. Why wouldn't he when he grew up with nothing? Flexing just didn't compute to him.

"You up, Ma," Self told Miss Johnson since it was her turn to drive. He stuffed the drugs under the driver's seat so she could claim it if they got caught. He'd agreed to pay her the five-thousand dollar discount he'd gotten from Rich. It was a win-win since she would turn around and give it back for drugs.

"Damn, I can smell that shit!" she exclaimed and passed gas from the excitement. "I may need a little hit just to..."

"Lil' hit my ass! Not until we get home safe and sound," Self cut in.

"Oh, okay!" she pouted.

Bad Ass pouted too in the backseat since he couldn't get any more head or smoke any weed.

Chapter 9

"Man, I hate to leave this place," Meisha sighed once she accepted she was actually awake. This was their last morning in Belize, it was time to go.

"Me, too," Trigga admitted with a deep sigh of his own.

For the last two weeks they'd relaxed like they were on vacation instead of on the run. Technically, the world thought Cameisha was dead so no one was looking for her. Still, she had done too much dirt and shed too much blood to stop looking over her shoulder.

"One for the road?" she asked, wrapping her hand around his morning erection. It throbbed his response and got even harder.

Cameisha threw her leg over his body to mount him. He moaned as she rubbed his swollen head between her vaginal lips. Once she was good and slippery, she slid down until his penis reached her cervix. Now it was Trigga's turn to grip the sheets and hold on as she rough rode him. She came a few miles later with a grunt and tipped over, out of breath. Trigga used the puddle left on his dick to stroke himself to an orgasm of his own. It didn't take long since she'd taken him right to the edge.

After a joint shower, they packed the few clothes they'd acquired and left the room. Rude Boy and Rosa were kissing and giggling in the dining room when they arrived. They both smiled when their guests came in but stopped when they noticed their bags.

"You guys leaving?" Rude Boy asked as if they'd only arrived five minutes before. Rosa's mouth turned down into a frown at seeing her new friend leaving.

"Yeah. He's moving much better now so it's time to move on," Meisha replied. She wanted to say they would be back or invite them to Brazil but left it off. It wasn't true, anyway. This would be the last time they saw each other.

The two couples made small talk until the taxi arrived to take them to the airport. No matter how good fake documents looked, the owner still knows that they're fake. Both Cameisha and Trigga held their breaths when they presented them to the ticket agent. She was more concerned with the pictures on the money than their passports.

Trigga gave Cameisha's hand a victory squeeze when they were safely seated on the plane. She, however, wouldn't be satisfied until they were in the air. She finally exhaled when the remove seatbelt light came on.

"Whew!" she exclaimed and placed a hand on her growing belly. Judging by her last period, she figured she was about three months or so.

"Told you we was straight," Trigga chuckled. "Hope this baby head ain't as big as yours! You gon' need an E-Section instead of a C-Section!"

"I know you ain't talking 'bout nobody's head..."

****

Cameisha and Trigga were still snapping on each other when they got off the plane in Brazil. The jokes eased the fear and uncertainty of being on another continent. A shrill shriek caused a slight panic amongst some travelers but it brought a smile to Meisha's face.

"There's my grandbaby!" Grandma Diedra shouted when the couple came into view.

"Grandma!" Meisha shouted back. She braced herself for the violence of a grandma hug that didn't come.

"Cameisha, are you pregnant?" Grandma Diedra demanded despite the obvious.

"Uh...yeah!" she cheered, proudly sticking her stomach out even further. "And this is my ba- um, fiancé, Tarvious.

"Pleased to meet you, ma'am," Trigga said, extending his hand in the direction which he heard the voice come from.

"Likewise, I'm sure," she said, shaking his hand while looking into his eyes. She frowned curiously and preceded to wave her hand in front of his face.

"Um... I can't see but...um...I can feel your hand in front of my face."

"I'm sorry, honey. I was just..."

"Buggin'!" Meisha cackled. "Take us to the house. I can't wait to see it!"

****

With the combined efforts of Killa and Cameron, the family had built a compound near the beach. It had several bungalows for privacy but everyone preferred to stay together in the main house. To Cameisha's surprise, her friend was outside when they pulled up.

"Sincerity! Girl, what you doing down here?" she shouted as she ran to embrace her friend.

"Girl, that damn Yolo, again!" she fussed and led her away to fill her in.

"Come on in, young man," Grandma Diedra said, giving him her elbow. "I'll show you to your room. It's down the hall from Cameisha's."

"Okay, thanks," he laughed.

Later that evening, the extended family all sat on the deck for dinner. Sincerity's son Xavier chatted with Trigga while Cameisha held little Rico. Diedra was delighted to have all the company so she went all out. They sat down to a seven course meal and conversation.

"So, what's your plans now that you're dead?" Grandma laughed.

"Just glad to be alive. I'm just going to live," she replied. "I gotta get to the bank and check on those accounts."

"I wouldn't. We got plenty of money and everything is already paid for," Diedra said, waving her arms around the lavish compound. "You don't ever need a penny for anything."

"I feel you but...I...um," Cameisha stammered. It is very hard to explain emotions like love, lust or greed, so she never found the words she'd been searching for. "It's so beautiful down here!"

"Mmhm," Grandma hummed. She knew her grandchild well enough to know that she was going to see about that money.

****

"You sure you don't mind?" Sincerity repeated before leaving the kids with Grandma.

"Ask me again," she dared. "Go 'head, ask me one mo' time!"

"Okay!" she laiughed and held her hands up in surrender. She knew the woman wouldn't mind but just wanted to be polite. "Meisha wants to do a little shopping. Poor girl had to walk away from all her belongings."

"Mmhm," Diedra repeated. She knew good and well that girl was going to that bank.

Trigga rode in the backseat shifting his head in every direction. He missed his vision in general but hated not being able to see the sounds and smells of the strange new world. Cameisha stared at the lush greenery until they reached the modern city.

"Wow, this looks like New York! Kinda," she exclaimed.

"Kinda," Sincerity agreed. The high end shops put her in the mind of downtown Manhattan, but the voices spoke a mix of Portuguese and Spanish.

"Oh, look! That's the same bank as the accounts!" Cameisha sang as pointed at the International Bank of Brazil. It sounded phony to her, too, because it was.

"I'll be in the Gucci store," Sincerity said, knowing she was going inside.

Who could blame her curiosity? Her dope father gave her numbered bank books before faking his own death. She babysat the books for years wondering what riches were inside. Could be a little, could be a lot. She was about to find out today.

"Okay, I'll just be a minute," she said, and helped Trigga from the backseat. They walked arm in arm on the marble floor until they reached a waiting area. "Wait here."

"Why don't I just wait here?" Trigga said so it would be his idea.

"Good idea, bae," she said and guided him into the chair. She put a little sway in her hips just in case his sight came back. It didn't but the click clack of her heels made him smile.

"English, Spanish or Portuguese?" the pretty teller requested when Cameisha arrived at her station. She had her pegged as an American and was proved right when she replied.

"English, please," she said as she placed the bank books on the counter. She just knew she was about to be embarrassed when she asked, "Can you please tell me my balance?"

"Okay, let's see here..." the woman replied in perfect English she'd learned while in college in America. The acting courses also paid off, allowing her to keep a straight face despite the warning flashing on her screen. "With accrued interest, eight point one. I need updated info please."

"Eight what?" Cameisha asked with a confused frown as she filled out the forms.

"Million. Eight million, one hundred five thousand dollars."

"Oh, okay," she replied nonchalantly even though her knees buckled and she felt like she had to pee. "I'll just withdraw ten thousand, U.S."

"But of course," she nodded and made the transaction. She returned the customer's smile as she handed over the money and watched her as she left until she was out of sight. Once Cameisha was gone, the teller grabbed her phone.

"Hola, Concepción! Are you ready to go to dinner with me?" the bank president asked when he took her call. He'd been trying to fuck her since the day she started working at the bank. Actually, that's why he'd hired her. Fuck her degree and her trilingual skills. The brunette beauty had a set of nice big titties and a tight little ass.

"No, sir. I don't think your wife would approve," she spat back. It was phony since she was definitely going to fuck him. He was just going to have to offer more than the dinners and chump change he'd been offering. "But I just had a customer access a Stein account."

"Stein! Who? When?" he asked, jumping to his feet. The late American attorney had opened several accounts years ago. None had been touched in over a decade. All held millions in drug money.

"Tywanna Rice..." she said, reading the form Cameisha had filled out with her new identity.

The bank manager hung up the second she finished. He picked the phone back up immediately and dialed. "Hola! There's been activity on a Stein account!" he blurted.

"Perfect," came the reply in perfect English. He wrote down the customer's information and nodded. It was just perfect. Perfect timing.

Chapter 10

"A-yo, you gon' help me with this shit or nah?" Self yelled up the stairs.

"I'm coming!" Bad Ass shouted back and giggled at his double entendre. Not only was he about to come downstairs to help cook, cut and bag crack, he was also about to cum down Miss Johnson's throat.

"Mm hm," the woman nodded. The extra movement of her head was all it took to get the teen off. She clamped down and held him in place until he stopped shivering and shaking.

"Damn, you got some good ass head!" Bad Ass announced.

"And y'all got some good ass dope, so come on with it!" she demanded, doing her hoola hoop dance.

"I gotcha, ma. We 'bout to cook up now," he said and hopped down the stairs to the kitchen where Self had just got to work. Bad Ass donned a mask and joined in. "Where yo' girl at?"

"At the mall getting baby stuff. You know she can't be 'round here while we cookin' up," Self replied. He suddenly wondered why he had her here in all the action anyway. They had taken over the apartment so it was time to get another spot to lay their heads. He was violating one of the ten crack commandments by shittin' were he ate.

"What?" Bad Ass asked, seeing his friend's brow burrowed from deep thought.

"Huh? Nothing. Sup with you and Miss Johnson? That yo' girl now?" Little Self cracked and cracked up as they cooked the crack up.

"Well, I am in a relationship with her tonsils," he laughed. "Yo, ma got some good ass head! That shit run in the family or nah?"

It took Self a couple of seconds to process the inappropriate question. That was only because he tried to spin it a few different ways on the strength of their friendship. That was why he waited a few more seconds to answer in a civil tone. "Yo, Angel is my girl. 'Bout to be my child's mother. She ain't no jump off, side chick or rec. My girl, B," he said clearly and evenly.

"Understood. My bad, bruh," Bad Ass said sincerely. He would never disrespect his friend on purpose. Little Self was the only one left on the planet that could trust him and that he could trust.

"We good," he said, accepting the pound and hug. They were more than good since they opted to sell the three kilos in strictly dimes. A lesson they'd learned directly form the Dope Girl herself.

They doubled their investment and flipped it again. At first, only the Eastwyck Crew could work but the drought caused by the entire Salazar Clan getting blown up was pushing the prices up. It was time to move up.

****

"I still don't think we should fuck with them cats," Self contemplated out loud. Lil C and Git from Glenwood had made a real humble appeal for work but he wasn't feeling it.

"Why not? I'ma tax them a grand an ounce. C.O.D, no credit, and no consignment," Bad Ass replied.

"Say no more," he assured. "I'm 'bout to go over and holla at Suge now. I'll see what they talkin' 'bout when I'm there."

"You ain't shit!" Little Self cracked. Suge was the ex-girlfriend of the late Flip.

"Told you I was gonna fuck they girls! I already smashed Nicky. Now it's Suge's turn!"

Suge was a short, bowlegged hoodrat. The only thing stopping her from being pretty was her one cocked eye. It killed her self-esteem at a young age. Now she wore the skimpiest of clothing to direct attention from it. It worked like a charm.

"Damn! I can see that rabbit from here," Bad Ass cheered as he pulled into the apartment complex. Suge had her shorts pulled tightly up into her crotch, forming a stop sign. Every dude who saw it stopped to holla.

Bad Ass stifled a laugh at the dope boys standing around with no dope. Some were losing weight from not eating since they got cut off. It was Flip and Flop who were actually responsible and they'd paid for it.

"Sup, yo?" Bad Ass asked Git from his window.

The baby-faced teen cracked a crooked smile and came over. "You, my nigga. Y'all decide to put a nigga on yet? I'm good, money!" he said, selling himself so he could get some dope to sell.

"Yeah, I'ma fuck with y'all," he said, feeling important. "Long as y'all keep it one hun'red, we all good!"

"Then we good then!" Git shot back and gave him some dap.

Lil C had just walked up on the tail end, but the smiling faces filled him in. "What he talking 'bout?" the newcomer asked, watching Suge hop her fine brown ass in his car. The only reason he'd never touched her was because they had the same grandmother. Half of the apartment complex was related in one way or another.

"A band for an onion," Git replied, watching Bad Ass leave with the local jump off. He had just jumped off in her last night himself since she wasn't his cousin.

"That's that bullshit!" Lil'C lamented. They had been paying six-fifty when Cameisha ran the show. They could still make over two thousand in the nickel and dime traffic of the trap.

"Yeah, but ain't no choice. Not yet, anyway. Soon as something else come up, I'ma see 'bout that nigga. He ain't getting away with killing my cousins," Flip and Flop's kin vowed.

****

"This is so nice!" Angel cheered and bounced as the agent showed the family their new apartment. The upscale Dunwoody area seemed like another planet than Decatur. She didn't see any junkies, dope boys or liquors.

"It is," Self agreed because it was, not to mention he didn't see a single police car. Most of the cops were back in Decatur with the junkies and dope boys.

"Mmhm," Angel's mother agreed. The lease would have to go in her name so they had to take her along. Of course, Self would break her off but offered an extra eight-ball if she didn't speak. All they got out of her was, "Mmhm."

"Two bedrooms, eight-hundred square feet, pool..." the agent rambled on needlessly. The family was sold from the security gate. "...one thousand a mouth, security deposit..."

"She'll take it!" Angel proclaimed. The party moved back to the leasing office to fill out the paperwork for the lease. Luckily, street credit doesn't show on credit reports so Miss Johnson had no problem getting a lease. The problem came when Little Self pulled a big roll of cash from his pocket.

"Oh no," the rental agent laughed. Her pink cheeks turned rosy red at the sight of greenbacks.

"Oh, my son-n-law is just giving me the cash so I can get the money orders," Miss Johnson cut in. It broke the deal but earned her an extra eight-ball instead.

"Uh...yeah," he replied. He didn't get it quite yet but he would. He was growing up quickly but still had much to learn. At least he was trying to learn. Unlike Bad Ass, who was only trying to learn new positions.

****

"Dang, Ma!" Bad Ass shouted as Suge rode him sideways. He propped himself up on his elbows and watched the show.

Suge had a huge vagina from multiple childbirths and multiple sexual partners. At eighteen, she had a forty-five-year-old woman's vagina. Still, it was warm and comfy as an old pair of slippers. They both faked an orgasm so they could move on to other things.

Suge planned to buy a few treats with the change she'd earned from this trick. Between buy one, get one free shoes and dollar store tops, she could get a whole new wardrobe with the hundred dollars Bad Ass came off.

Meanwhile, he had to go check the traps. That meant collecting what they were owned and re-supplying the dope. He pulled the empty condom off, flushed it down the toilet, washed his dick in the sink and then got dressed.

"We need to hangout again sometime," Suge offered when they got into the car. The cheap clothes and shoes wouldn't last long so she would need to go shopping again.

"Yeah," he replied while mentally shaking his head 'no'. She was a sexy little hoodrat but the sex was wack. He lit a blunt to distract her from trying to lock in a date. It worked and they rode the rest of the way in silence.

"Who is that?" Bad Ass asked, seeing a young woman at the bus stop in front of the apartments. He knew the face but couldn't recall from where.

"That's Kisha," Suge said in a condescending tone. "That's the one who baby got kilt when some niggas shot up the 'partments. Kilt my baby daddy, too."

"Word?" he said, watching Kisha's ass as she climbed up on the bus. It didn't even register that he was the one who'd shot up the apartments. All he knew was she had a fat ass.

Chapter 11

"So, how's married life treating you? I ain't never getting married. Shit, I'm married to the Mob," Bad Ass rambled through the mask he wore as he and Self cooked up more crack.

Masks had to be worn full-time now since the apartment was now a full-fledged smoke house. With Angel safely tucked away across town, junkies could even sit there and smoke their dope. That allowed Miss Johnson to put a tax on each rock sold.

"Dope," he said. That one word answer actually spoke volumes. He and Angel had furnished the apartment with all the extras. Their audio-visual system was great but what he liked most were the pots and pans. He got good home cooking every night after a long day of trapping.

"That's what's up my ni-" he replied and was cut off by Self's phone. Even he knew Angel's ringtone by now and knew his partner was going to take the call.

"It's time!" Angel shouted as soon as he took the call. Her water had broken, creating a sense of urgency.

"I'm on my way!" he said and hung up. He barged out of the kitchen and through the living room. Angel's mom had her chest stuck out while holding on to a hit of crack for dear life. She took sips of air trying to keep it in. "Angel 'bout to have the baby. You coming?"

Self shook his head when she shook her head. He could never understand the pull of addiction. When people take their desires as their god, all else goes out the window.

****

"Don't go, just stay here," Mrs. Ward pleaded to Mr. Ward. They'd recently celebrated their twentieth wedding anniversary so she knew him well enough to know what that look in his eyes meant.

"Just a drive, to get some fresh air," Robert assured Sherry. He'd just celebrated an anniversary of his own, a year of being clean.

The married man had had a two-year affair with a crack pipe. He never once indulged in the crack whores that came with the territory, but he'd cheated on his wife nonetheless. Cocaine is just another false god, but it's a jealous lord. It had demanded all his time, energy and money.

Sherry Ward was the definition of a ride or die chick, and had stood by her man. She paid what he didn't pay and made excuses to friends and family. Even their adult children had given up on him, but not her.

"You sure you don't want to stay?" she purred affectionately, hoping to lure him between her legs. That would be a win for both of them since she was feeling a bit horny. He paused at the sight of her crotch and then continued to getting fully dressed.

"I'm okay, Sherry. I got it. I'm just going for a drive," he said and left the room.

It had been a year since his last blast and that was good. So good, even the devil congratulated him. Then convinced him he that he should go out and celebrate, have a drink, maybe two.

Mr. Ward rolled down his window and inhaled the fresh night's air. He held it deep within his being just like he used to inhale crack vapors. He even blew it out as if it was smoke. He had no particular destination in mind, yet his muscle memory steered the car towards Glenwood Road. That's where he used to cop his rocks.

"Won't hurt to look," the devil suggested as he neared the apartment complex. The brisk activity showed that the trap was booming. The twenty-dollar bill in his pocket seem to get hot and burn his leg.

"Yeah, I can look. Ain't no harm in looking," he agreed and pulled in.

"Hey! Hey!" a skinny addict yelled and flailed her arms as Robert eased into the parking lot. She was so frantic that he pulled to a stop to see what she wanted. She grabbed the door handle and was in the passenger's seat in a flash. "Pull over there!"

"Do I know you?" he wondered as he complied to the demand.

"I'm Nika," she explained as if that explained it. In a flash, she snatched his dick from his pants and lowered her head on to his lap. He was so confused by the sudden sex act that his body didn't respond, not at first anyway. But soon her hot, wet suction gave him a rock hard erection.

Robert watched the drug activity instead of the activity in his lap. The happy faces of the customers meant the dope boys had some good dope. His stomach churned in anticipation. He may just have to get a little blast. Just a little one, that wouldn't hurt. His thoughts were interrupted by an eruption in his loins.

"Mmhm," Nika nodded and hummed as he skeeted in her mouth. She waited until he'd finished spasming and then swallowed it all at once. She politely put his dick back where she'd gotten it from and stuck her empty palm out. "Twenty please."

"I...um...well...okay," he stammered. He had decided to use that bill on a rock but now had to pay for the service.

Nika took the money and sprinted to the dope boys. The twenty had been his only cash on hand and he didn't carry an ATM card so he had to abandon his plan. He'd been saved by a blowjob.

****

"I'm here, baby. I... aww, man!" Little Self sighed when he entered the hospital room. He'd wanted to witness the birth of their child, but Angel held already held a bundle of joy on her bosom when he arrived.

"Here go your daddy," the new mother sang softly to the infant.

Self's legs felt heavy as he crossed the room to meet his child. The weight of responsibility bogged him down immediately. That's a good thing, though. That meant he'd accepted his duties as a daddy, a notion that never registered with some men.

"W-what is it?" he asked as he looked at the child. It had a head full of shiny black hair and skin the color right in between his tan and her pretty black.

"It..." she giggled, "is your daughter, Samantha Monae Williams."

Little Self smiled widely at the familiar sounding name. He was born Samuel Williams himself. His ability to take care of himself at an early age had earned him the moniker he went by. Now, still at an early age, he had two more people to take care of. His chest puffed out involuntarily as he mentally accepted the challenge.

"Nah, I don't know how," he reeled as she extended their child towards him.

"Sure you do," she assured him. Angel grabbed her phone and took pictures of father and daughter for her social media accounts. "Did you see my mama?"

"Huh?" he asked instead of lying. "Call her and I'll go pick her up."

"Naw, she probably too high. I don't want my baby to see what I had to see. Can we move somewhere? Somewhere for away, like...Texas or California?" she pleaded. The slums of Atlanta were no different than the slums of New York so Self nodded his head.

"Yeah, ma, we can go. I just gotta get our money right," he replied. An hour later, he left the hospital to do just that.

****

"Man, you sound fuckin' crazy!" Bad Ass chided when his partner filled him in on his exit plan. He was a dope boy for life and had no other plans except to get rich or die trying.

"Guess so, cuz I'm doing it," he said, sticking to his guns. "Now you help me get my money up and then this whole shit is yours."

Bad Ass liked the sound of being the man by himself. He nodded along with the vision of not having to split half the proceeds. His twenty-thousand a week would double to forty. Then he could take over more apartment complexes and double that. Get a good South American connect and triple that. Then...

"Yo, B, you should see the look on your face!" Self laughed at his friend. The quest for money and power had spread a look of lust on his handsome face.

"Whatever. Anyway, I got a date. 'Bout to take Kisha to a movie."

"You? A date?" Self laughed. "Not Mr. 'Fuck a Bitch'.

"Well, I'm still gon' fuck the bitch! We just gonna catch a movie first," he explained. He pulled out a strip of paper with name 'Kisha' on it and dialed the number.

Chapter 12

"I...um...I'm about to go...um..." Cameisha stammered.

"Shopping?" Grandma Diedra helped out with a knowing laugh. All the girl did was eat and shop. Even deep into her last trimester, she tore the high end stores a new one.

"Yeah, pick up a few things for the baby," she replied and put a hand on her huge belly just in case anyone wondered which baby she was referring to.

"Mmhm," came the reply. Diedra knew her granddaughter found a reason to hit the bank at least a couple of times a month. She had several hundred thousand in cash in her room. Not to mention all the stuff she claimed was for the baby. The child wasn't even born yet and had a Prada this a Gucci that. Now the baby needed a new Benz.

Cameisha had mixed emotions about being rich. On one hand, she loved being able to buy whatever she wanted but she had no one to show off in front of. Sincerity would say 'ooh, that's nice', Grandma could care less and Trigga couldn't see shit. What good was getting all dressed up with nowhere to go? That's why she had plans on a trip as soon as she gave birth. It was a stupid plan, but a plan nonetheless.

"I'm ready," Trigga announced as he came out of the room. In the months that they'd been down there, he'd memorized his surroundings. He knew exactly how many steps in any direction it took to get to any destination.

"Yes, you are, handsome!" she cheered, seeing her man dressed in a tasteful linen suit and croc loafers.

He smiled at the compliment and had to take her word for it. "Thank you," he replied, stroking the long platinum and diamond chain hanging from his neck. He too wished he could show it off to someone. This was the pride before the fall that the Bible speaks of.

****

"There they go, Josito," Carlos said when Cameisha pulled out of the gated compound. They'd followed her to the bank a little while ago, and had been following her ever since.

"I have eyes," Josito shot back. They'd both been assigned the task of watching the girl and they both wanted to be the boss. He put the car in gear and began to follow.

"Not so close! Slow down!" the backseat driver demanded from the passenger's seat. Josito sucked his teeth in reply, but did slow down a little bit.

All of Trigga's other senses had been enhanced since his lights had went out. Not just his hearing, touch and sense of taste, but also his intuition. He felt someone behind them and looked to where he knew the mirror was. Of course, he couldn't see anything but he sure could feel it. He'd been feeling it for a while.

For the rest of the day, the two henchmen followed the couple. Cameisha bought more matching jewelry and shoes for her. All the clothes she bought were in the size seven she planned to get back down to as soon as she dropped her load.

The thugs couldn't afford to eat at the swank outdoor patio the couple dined at, so they grabbed a bite from a food cart as they kept an eye on them from the street.

"I gotta go to the States after I...um...have the baby," Cameisha said. She waited until he had a mouthful of seafood alfredo before she spoke so that he couldn't. "Got...um...some stuff to check on, youknowwhatI'msaying,"

"Mm-mm," he shook his head. He didn't know what she was saying. They'd made a clean getaway. All they had to do now was just live. If only it could be that simple.

"Yeah, Aqua, Jackie and..." she rambled, making up excuses as she went along.

Meanwhile, Trigga forced down un-chewed shrimp and scallops so he could speak. "Hell naw! You dead, so stay dead! We straight down here. Why take a chance going back?" he reasoned.

Cameisha knew good and damn well he was right but she was Cameisha. "You right. I'm dead, which means nobody is looking for me. No one is going to pay me any attention when I go home," she replied.

They went back and forth through the rest of their meal. Trigga paid for the hundred dollar lunch with two hundred dollar bills.

"Thank you! Thank you!" the happy waitress smiled and bounced at the gracious gratuity.

"Look it!" Carolos said when Cameisha took one final sip from her straw. He rushed over and collected it as soon as they stepped away from the table. It would be tested for DNA to see just who Tywanna Rice really was. The boss' extensive contacts in the States could find no record of her.

****

The debate about Cameisha going stateside had turned into a full-fledged argument by the time they reached the car dealership. They salesman frowned curiously as they bickered during the test drive of a 2016 G-Wagon. Even while arranging payment, they went back and forth. As a result, the ride home in the luxury truck was made in complete silence, except for his pouts and her teeth sucking.

Trigga barged through the living room and straight into the bedroom. The heat required a midday shower so he rushed under the water.

"Oh Lord, what you do to that man?" Sincerity asked, shaking her head. She knew if she was Cameisha's man, she would have choked her smart mouthed ass a long time ago.

"Nothing. He'll be alright," she said, following him into the room. She knew she had a smart mouth and knew she went too far. Now it was time to make it up.

Cameisha waited until she heard the shower cut off before getting into position. She stripped out of her maternity clothes and kneeled doggy style on the bed.

Trigga was naked except for the disgusted frown on his face when he stepped into the room. He only took two steps before he stopped and sniffed the air. Not only could he smell the sweetness of her vagina from across the room, he could feel its heat also. His dick jumped to fully erect as he crossed the room.

"Mmm," Cameisha moaned as he rubbed his dick head on her swollen lips. The friction caused her to bust a nut before he'd even entered her.

"Make...me...damn...sick!" he growled while sinking into her hot pocket.

"Mmhm, I know," she giggled and squeezed.

He slid slowly in and out, making her cum once more. Too bad he couldn't see all that good creamy lotion she'd coated his dick with. When the feeling got too intense, he pulled out and used it to stroke himself as he came all over her back.

"Eww!" Cameisha squealed when she felt several globs of semen land on the back of her head. "My hair!"

"My bad," he giggled because he wasn't sorry. He led her back into the bathroom and under the warm water. Cameisha saw the opportunity to further her agenda and squatted down to take advantage of it.

"Baby...I...just...need...a couple...of...weeks," she pleaded in between kissing, licking and twirling her tongue on his dick. She felt his knees buckle when she took him inside her mouth and knew she had him.

She grabbed his hips to steady herself and went to town. Soon his hips thrusted as he slammed in and out of her mouth. She knew what it meant when his body began to shiver but didn't move. She clamped down and took all he had to offer. A lot was riding on it, so she made sure he heard her when she swallowed.

"Shit! A'ight! You win! A couple of weeks," he relented.

Proof that good head can cost a life.

Chapter 13

"What you gon' do if you get me pregnant?" Kisha wanted to know once Bad Ass finished cumming in her. They'd been having unprotected sex for weeks now.

"You straight," he replied as he rolled off her. It wouldn't bother him if she did. He couldn't help but admire his partner Self becoming a daddy. Not to mention he was digging the girl.

"Okay, I'm straight!" she mocked and laughed. That cute laugh that made the goon smile. Her tone turned serious and she twisted her lips in thought. "I miss my son so much!"

"I know, shorty," he said, scooping the crying girl into his arms. "That's fucked up. Who would shot a kid with a shotgun?"

"I'on know," she sobbed. "It wasn't the buckshot that killed him though. The autopsy said it was a forty-five ACP. Whatever that means."

"Say word!" he reeled. He knew exactly what it was. It was the type of round that came from a Mac-10. That meant he was responsible for the child's death. If he had a conscience, it probably would have fucked with it. He didn't, so he lit the blunt and took a pull.

Kisha's soft sobs subsided when Bad Ass passed the weed. They smoked, kissed and then fucked once more. She spread her legs wide and tilted her ass when he came in her once again. She didn't mind having a baby by him. Perhaps he would be a better father than Git was.

****

"Can I come with you?" Kisha asked when they awoke intertwined on the hotel bed the next morning. He had told her that he had to make a run to New York and she wanted in.

"Nah, it's a business trip. Just me and my man," he replied as he fondled her vagina to get it nice and wet so he could get one for the road.

"Man," she pouted and spread her legs a little wider for him.

Once she was slick and slippery, he rolled on top and slid inside of her. "Man is right!" he exclaimed. It seemed like the pussy was tighter than the night before. It wasn't, he was just getting whipped.

Kisha squeezed her walls and rubbed his back as he humped. He threw his hips into overdrive and came with a grunt. He added more semen into her cervix, not caring about the result.

Kisha pouted as Bad Ass drove her home. They were met by contemptuous glances as they pulled into the apartment complex. The hoes were mad that he didn't scoop them up anymore and the dudes were hot about him having another one of their women. Not to mention he was in yet another car, wearing yet another chain.

Even Git was hot about him hitting his ex, despite him refusing to claim their child. He and Kisha went together for a year before she got pregnant. A baby meant responsibilities and the young thug wanted no parts of it.

"Don't let none of these niggas take it," Bad Ass said as he slipped his chain over her neck. "I don't wanna have to come shoo... Anyway, I'll see you when I get back."

"Okay," Kisha sang and hopped out. All eyes were on her as she floated happily towards her building. The miserable people hated seeing her happy.

"Sup, yo?" Bad Ass greeted as he pulled over to the trap. He could care less how they were but did want them to see his new whip.

"It's all good, shawty," Lil-C replied, checking out the new looking used Audi. Git just glared from the sideline. "We gon' need some more work 'round here in a minute."

"We out now. Soon as we get straight, I'll fall through. Shit gone be twelve now, but it's all good," he replied.

"Twelve?" Git finally spoke. That was almost double what they had been paying just months back.

"It is what it is," Bad Ass replied smugly.

What it was was Richie Rich raising the price from eighteen-five to twenty grand. He could have explained that but Bad Ass was a smart ass. Plus, he liked sticking it to the crew from Glenwood. He was still too young to fully understand the dangers of disrespecting people. He would learn, though.

****

"Shit, we can cop two, split it fifty-fifty and still be straight," Self said as he drove towards New York. He'd wisely decided to rent a family-friendly minivan to blend in with traffic.

"Hmm?" Bad Ass asked from the backseat. Miss Johnson was bobbing her head up and down, distracting him.

"I said, even with cuz charging us twenty each, we can still eat," he explained. The flip should net five-hundred-grand, which meant a profit of a hundred and fifty grand each. He planned to add his to his savings so he could buy a happily-ever-after.

"Not bad," Bad Ass said. He had plans on fucking his up as soon as he got it. He had his eye on a Cadillac truck and a diamond earring the size of a ball of hail.

"Mmhm," Mama agreed with a mouthful of dick. A few more bobs of her head and she had a mouthful of cum. Bas Ass leaned back and drifted off to sleep.

"When you coming to see Samantha?" Self asked once they were technically alone. The baby was several months old and she hadn't been by the apartment yet.

"Huh?" she asked since she didn't have an answer. What she did know was that she didn't want to meet her first grandchild in that condition. For the first time in twenty years, she was tired of being a junkie. She just didn't know what to do about it.

Self just shook his head and kept driving.

Bad Ass woke up near Richmond, Virginia. He got another blowjob before it was his turn to drive. Self leaned back into the passenger's seat and stared out the window. He missed all the scenery from looking at his future. A few more flips and he was gone.

****

"Bad news, cuz-o," Rich exclaimed cheerfully as if he had said it was good news. That's because it was good for him, but for Self and Bad Ass not so much.

"What? Bruh, don't tell me you sold out! You knew we was coming! We just drove thirteen and a half hours and..."

"Chill, Lil Sammy! We got work, it's just, they thirty now. I can give you six for that two hunned," he cut in. He was just a middle man making a grand off each kilo he sold. Now, seeing his little cousin getting money, he had to tax him. It was Bad Ass's fault for wearing a different chain every time they came.

"First of all...that's six and a half for two-hundred grand," he said, doing the math on his phone. "And two, what kinda shit you on cuz?"

"Shit tight," he lied. "If you don't want it..."

"Nah, we'll take it. It's all good," Bad Ass cut in, pursing his lips. He didn't mind paying the extra since he'd just made up his mind to rob him.

The two-hundred-thousand they brought bought six-point-six kilos of cocaine. It was pure this time but Richie Rich made up his mind to put a ten percent cut on the next one. Maybe twenty since they couldn't do anything about it.

There goes that pride again so a fall was soon to follow.

Chapter 14

"A-yo, I know I told y'all twelve but it's gonna be thirteen-fifty," Bad Ass told Git and company when he came to resupply them with ounces of crack. Again, he could have explained the price increase, but again, he decided to be cocky.

"You really going too far, shawty," Lil-C warned. Bad Ass was too arrogant to hear the danger in his tone.

"Real talk, shawty, you acting like we work for you," Git seconded.

"Shit, y'all can. I'll give y'all three off the 'G' and y'all ain't gotta spend your own money," he said, despite his and Self's agreement not to front them any work.

"We'll see," Git said and bought a couple of ounces instead of a few like he'd planned. No sooner did Bad Ass leave than they began to plot on him. "We gon' follow him to the stash spot and get all that shit."

"Sho' nuff. Then I'ma put a bullet in that nigga's head," Lil-C growled.

Nika rushed over to the trap with a freshly squeezed twenty-dollar bill. She still had semen on her breath as she purchased two of the dime-sized rocks. She frowned at the obvious reduction in size and protested.

"Y'all getting chincy 'round this bitch!" she lamented.

"Here, give 'em back then!" Lil-C demanded, trying to hand her money back to her.

"Nuh uh!" she protested, turning her body away from the money. She sucked her teeth, dislodging some more semen and stomped off. The smaller rocks meant there were more dicks that had to be sucked. She was happy to see a familiar car ease into the complex. She ran over and hopped in before it could come to a complete stop.

"Hey there," Robert Ward greeted. He had been venturing out at night for a couple of weeks now. He still hadn't gotten high but he enjoyed the excitement of an illicit blowjob in the family's car.

Nika was never one for formalities, so she quickly got him inside of her mouth. He pulled over into a parking spot so he could lean back and enjoy the hot mouth. Nika wrapped her small hand around his shaft and worked it in unison with her mouth. The harmonious symphony got him off in a matter of minutes. Now he could relax enough to sit at home.

"Twenty bucks," she requested after adding his semen to the collection already in her stomach.

"My pleasure," he smiled and handed over the money. He almost had tacit approval for the blowjobs since the first time. Sherry had drilled him so hard when he got in about if he'd gotten high or not that he'd come clean about the blowjob. She was so relieved that he hadn't used drugs that she said, 'oh, okay,' and left it alone.

"You mind if I get a lil' bump?" Nika asked and pulled out her pipe. No words came out so she went on and fixed up a hit.

Robert gulped loudly as he watched her break one of the dimes in half and load her straight shooter. At that moment, it was as dangerous as any gun. More dangerous, in fact, because it's a slow, painful, embarrassing death. His eyes lit up with the lighter and he actually inhaled along with her as she pulled the poison through the pipe and into her lungs.

"Can I hit it?" someone in the car said. Robert glanced in the mirror to see if anyone was in the backseat but there wasn't.

"Hmph," Nika said, holding the smoke in her lungs as she passed the smoking pipe.

A year's worth of sobriety vanished in an instant when he pulled on the pipe.

Nika let him start the other half of the dime. She could tell by how he hit it that he knew what he was doing. As clean cut as he was, she just knew he had plenty of cash to spend. She would hold on to her last rock and money and let him buy the next round.

"Give me another twenty so I can get some more," she suggested.

"That's all I had," he said with mixed emotions. Sure, he had fucked up but luckily, he didn't have any more money to make things worse. She twisted her lips up at him and hopped out. He wouldn't be smoking up all her shit.

"Oh, Lawd," Robert said to himself as he drove home. He was in trouble and he knew it. The floodgates of addiction were now wide open and he didn't know if he had the strength to fight it. He sat in his driveway for thirty minutes before gaining the courage to face his wife.

"You okay?" Sherry Ward asked, seeing the diluted look of distress on her husband's face.

The weak smile couldn't mask his anguish. "Huh?" he stalled. "Yeah, fine. You okay?"

"Mmhm. Musta got another blowjob," she huffed. She really didn't mind since she didn't like to do it. Anniversary, birthday, and maybe New Year's, but not every damn day.

"Huh? Nah, I," he replied and left off all the lies that would've followed, "I'm just tired."

"So, go to bed!" she shot back. "I'll be up after my movie."

Robert went upstairs and took a cold shower. His dick was already shriveled up from the dope and the cold water only made it worse. He could only hope his wife wasn't watching Lifetime and came up wanting some. He had none to give her at the moment.

Chapter 15

"Huh?" Trigga frowned in the darkness as he felt his leg get wet. "Meisha? Meisha, did you pee the bed?"

"No," she replied, feeling the same liquid as he did.

"Then, what's this?" he asked, sitting up in bed. He could feel a puddle between her legs and it was spreading.

"Not pee," she replied. She knew that her water had broken but she was not ready. Being pregnant was cool, she didn't mind peeing every few minutes or the swollen ankles. She had no problem at all being a mommy, but squeezing a baby out of her vagina, now that was a different story. "I'm in labor."

"Well, get up! We gotta get you to the hospital!" Trigga exclaimed as he bolted off the bed.

"No, I'm good. Maybe next week," she suggested then got rocked with a contraction.

"Grandma Diedra!" Trigga shouted and took off to go get her. He had the layout of the house committed to memory for walking. It was not the same running.

"Poor fella gonna kill himself," Cameisha laughed as she watched Trigga play pinball with his body against the walls.

"Girl, why haven't you moved? That baby is coming!" Diedra fussed when she arrived followed by Sincerity.

"Don't punk out now!" Sincerity laughed. She then helped Cameisha to her feet. "It ain't that bad."

"It still hurts to have sex sometimes, I know a baby is bigger than a dick!" she fussed.

"Grandmother in the room," Grandma Diedra reminded. "Girl, they're going to numb you from the waist down. You won't feel a thing!"

****

"It's...a boy!" the doctor announced when the child slid completely out of his mother.

"Tarvious Jackson!" Trigga proudly proclaimed.

"Un, not!" Cameisha protested. "How about Cameron? Cameron Forrest-Jackson."

"Whatever," Trigga pouted. He felt slightly slighted and slightly punked but let it go.

The baby was cleaned, weighed and taken through other newborn baby stuff before being returned to his mother. The fake IDs the couple carried meant that they couldn't register him as an American child. She would have to worry about that later. Soon she would have much bigger problems on her hands.

Carlos smiled happily at the birth of the baby boy. He had no idea who the woman he and Josito were assigned to follow was but rooted for her. Still, he had a job to do, so he went to report the latest development.

"Ay dios mío," he said, hoping he wouldn't have to kill her, him or the baby. He would, but hoped he wouldn't have to.

"Very well," the voice on the phone replied, sounding happy himself. The boss was delighted at the news of a healthy baby boy having been brought into the world. He had ten of them himself. "Well, let her enjoy him and we'll see her in a few weeks."

****

Robert Ward had of history of fucking up his paychecks. Back in his addiction hey-day, he would leave work at lunchtime on payday and not be seen again until the money was completely spent. He would then show up tired, hungry and broke. It wasn't uncommon for him to reek of cigarettes, alcohol, pussy and pee.

His wife, Sherry, had signed up for better or worse. The better was a lot better and helped her get through the worse. She loved her husband dearly and he had been a great husband, father and provider until addiction moved in with them. Not just into the house but into their martial bed as well. There were a many of nights when his drug use prevented him from achieving an erection, adding sexual frustration to her general frustration.

That was then and this was now. Now Robert would take his check to the bank at lunch and head back to work. Back then, his compassionate employer had started holding his checks for Mrs. Ward to come collect. It was an embarrassment for them both but not as embarrassing as losing their home and cars or sitting in the dark.

Robert sat as his desk with his mind bouncing every which way, like one of the super bouncy balls from a supermarket dispenser. The hit he took with Nika a week ago nagged at him every chance it got. He hadn't gone back since, hoping to save his sobriety.

"Earth to Bob!" Robert's supervisor called out, waving his hand in front of his face. He had been so deep in thought that he hadn't seen him enter his office.

"Oh, hey, Bill," he replied when he returned to the present.

"Payday, plus...quarterly bonuses!" he cheered and handed him his check. "An extra grand of 'she money'. Money 'she doesn't know about'. I'm getting myself a new set of golf clubs. What are you going to do with yours?"

"Oh, I don't know," Robert lied. He knew exactly what he was going to do with it. After a whispered conversation with the devil, it was decided that he would use the spare cash to get high. After a whole year of being clean and sober, he deserved it. It was extra money and wouldn't affect his household. Not to mention...

"Bob?" his boss asked again when he drifted off once more.

"I'm sorry. I...um...yeah," he stammered and stood. He was still mumbling as he rushed from the office.

The ride from downtown Atlanta to Glenwood Road in Decatur was a short one. It was made even shorter due to the trance he was in. The bulk of his paycheck was deposited safely in the bank. Bills would get paid on time and in full. The extra grand was in his pocket just in case he needed it.

Nika was standing on the curb in front of the complex trying to find a dick to suck. Not only would it put something in her empty stomach, it would also buy her a rock to fill her empty pipe. A yellow cum and crack stained smile spread on her face when she saw Robert Ward's car pull in.

The clean man had a clean car, a clean dick and he paid the twenty bucks to get it sucked. It beat sucking musty nut having dope boys' dicks for a crumb of crack. She rushed over as quickly as her skinny legs could so no other crack whore beat her to the punch. Lunch, actually.

"Whoa!" Robert shouted when he almost ran Nika down. He had locked his eyes on the dope boys in the trap and hadn't even seen her dart in front of the car.

"Hey! Pull over there," Nika said, pointing at an empty spot.

The man held her head as it bobbed up and down while keeping an eye on the trap. A tinge of fear crept in as he hoped that they wouldn't sell out before he finished. He had to concentrate on the blowjob to bring it to an end. He thrust his hips up to help it along.

"Mmhm," she nodded, feeling her mouth fill. It even tasted better than dope boys' cum since their diets consisted of chips, burgers, weed and pills. She tucked the shiny dick away with one hand and extended the other to be paid. Once she had the twenty in hand, she prepared to leave.

"Wait! Why don't you hang out with me?" he suggested. "I wanna cop a couple of rocks myself."

"Pull over to the trap. Lil-C got the fattest rocks," she said. He really didn't, he just cut them at angles that made them look larger than they were. "What you tryna spend?"

"Say, a hundred," he said since that's how much he'd separated for the excursion. The other nine hundred was to pay for a trip to Savannah for him and the Mrs.

"'Scuse me!" she giggled when the thought of all that dope made her pass gas. "Hey, Lil-C."

"Sup, shawty?" he asked, cocking his head curiously. He looked the driver over for traces of law enforcement but found none.

"Let me get a hunned slab!" she cheered. The hundred-dollar slab was a better buy than five twenty-dollar pieces. Usually, lower level dope boys would cop them and break them down for street sales.

Robert understood his cue and produced a crisp hundred. Both the dealer and the whore recognized the bill as being fresh form a bank. The both knew enough to know that there was more where that came from. They both planned on getting as many as they could out of the man.

"Let's get us a room," she suggested once the transaction was complete.

"Um...okay," he agreed. He had planned to get a room anyway, so why not have some company?

****

Robert removed his tie and dress shirt as soon as they stepped in the room. Nika pulled a straight shooter from her bra and kicked off her beat up tennis shoes. They had almost as may miles on them as her vagina.

"I go first since it's my pipe!" she declared as if it were a rule written somewhere. Crackheads have no rules and there certainly was no crackhead rule book.

"Um, okay," he agreed, even though he felt like he should go first since he did buy it. He broke off a piece of the rock and handed it over. He watched with glee as she took a deep pull. It was too much for her to take, so she no choice but to pass it.

Nika began to strip out of her shorts and tank top as she held the smoke in. The room filled with the odor of crawfish when her pissy panties came off. Her once shapely body now looked like a beanstalk. "Ooh! My pussy stank!" she reeled. "Save me some. I'll be back."

Once Robert heard the shower, he broke off a third of the rock and hid it in his sock. The drugs suggested he take his clothes off, too, so he did. He knew from experience that if he took one more hit, the chances of him getting an erection were slim to none. He began to pull on his penis so Nika returned to a rock hard erection.

"A'ight then!" Nika cheered at the hard dick. She knew exactly what to do with it and rushed onto the bed. She kneeled down with her ass in the air, but quickly changed her mind and flipped over on her back instead. The nimble addict grabbed the back of her knees and pulled her legs over her head.

Robert looked at the dusty bush over her plump vagina and climbed on the bed. A man would have to be high to enter her raw, but he was, so he did and fell all the way to the bottom.

For the next hour, the married man twisted, turned and fucked her in ways his wife would never allow. Forwards, backwards, sideways, the other side and finally, in the other hole. He could have gone on for another hour if not for all that dope demanding to be smoked.

"Argh!" he grunted and contorted his face while ejaculating on hers. She scrambled to get him in her mouth and milk him dry.

Nika popped up right behind him and joined him at the table. She didn't even bother to wipe the globs of semen away out of fear of missing her turn. It would be late Sunday evening when they finished smoking and drinking. Mrs. Ward was waiting in the den when he returned.

"Hey," she said with a weary sigh. Deep in her heart, she knew this day would come. She prayed that it wouldn't but knew that it would.

"Um...hey," he croaked. His voice was dry and strained from forty-eight hours of hot crack and menthol smoke. His penis itched on the inside from a dose of chlamydia and he was dog tired. "I was...um..."

"I know," she replied knowingly. She had been through it all before and knew what he would say. The only unanswered question was if she was willing to go through it all again.

Chapter 16

"Sup, cuz! I'ma need to come check you in a day or two!" Self said, dancing as he spoke. Why wouldn't he be doing his happy dance since the trap was booming? His cousin was taxing him at thirty for a kilo but he was still winning. He had three-hundred-thousand for ten more.

"Aw, shit, man. You ain't seen the news, B?" Richie Rich proclaimed while pointing at his T.V. The news wasn't even on but that didn't matter since he was lying anyway.

"Nah, what?" he asked dryly. Knowing his cousin the way he did, he knew some bullshit was forthcoming.

"Yo, the Dominicans just got knocked off with a whole boatload. The prices is fucked up now. I gotta get for...um, fifty each. I can let you get ten but they for the fiddy."

"It's like that, yo?" Little Self growled. His tone caused Bad Ass to take note and walk over.

"What?" his partner asked.

"Cuz talkin' about fifty each," Self said with his voice cracking form anger and sorrow.

"Let me see," Bad Ass said, reaching for the phone. He took a deep breath and exhaled before lifting the phone to his mouth. "Peach fam, what's this I hear about fifty each?"

"It's a drought, B. If y'all wasn't my peeps, I'd have to hit you for the sixty," he swore.

"A'ight, but since we are family, let us get them for say...forty-two each," he haggled.

"You killin' me, bruh!" Rich said dramatically. "Only cuz you my nigga! On the strength of you, my nigga!"

"Yo, I ain't..." Self protested until his partner shushed him.

"Okay. Un-huh. Sounds good. One," Bad Ass finished.

"A-yo, son, I'm not paying forty-two for a brick!" Self vowed.

"Me, either," he shot back.

The rest didn't need to be said since they both understood that he planned to rob him.

****

"My grandma," Self sighed as he, Bad Ass and Capo prepared for the ride to New York.

Bad Ass knew he was having second thoughts about the robbery. No one even tried to fool themselves into thinking that it wouldn't turn into a murder. You steal ten kilos from someone, you have to kill them. That's a wound that doesn't heal over time. That's an enemy for life. Rich and Self shared a grandmother, which raised the stakes.

"I got this," he said, letting him off the hook. "You need to go hit up Lil-C and them on Glenwood. I fronted them some work and..."

"I thought we...said we...wasn't doing that?" Little Self demanded.

"Yeah...uh...you was busy with the baby and shit, so I took care of it," he replied. It was a veiled shot at how much time his partner spent at home with his family.

Ironically, Kisha had just broken the news to him that she was pregnant. He was happy about having an heir since he'd expected to die young, but the streets still came first.

"A'ight, yo," Self sighed. He didn't have the strength to argue. His family was about to be in mourning.

****

"Damn, I shoulda brought ole Miss Johnson along for the ride," Bad Ass said as they reached the Carolina border.

"Yeah, she got some fiyah head!" Capo agreed from behind the wheel. Bad Ass twisted his lips and cut his eyes at him jealously. After all, he was in a relationship with her tonsils.

"Anyway," he said to change the subject. "You ready to get this money?"

"Hell yeah! Shit, I'ma come the fuck up off three bricks!" he cheered. The agreement was to split the ten kilo robbery between three of them but Bad Ass that Rich wasn't lying about having a hundred kilos. Capo didn't know it but he was staying in New York if he did.

Little Self was the voice of reason so his absence made it seem reasonable to smoke weed the whole trip up north. Never mind all the guns in the car. Bad Ass' bulletproof vest alone was enough for him to go to jail for since it was stolen police issue.

It took them just under thirteen hours to reach Harlem. Capo's head flicked left, right, up and down as he took in the strange new world. His sightseeing tour ended when Bad Ass pulled to a stop a block away from Rich's building.

"You ready, B?" he asked as he pulled on his vest. A heavy sweatshirt covered but didn't conceal it.

"Not as ready as you!" he shot back. "Wish I had me a vest, too! You think shawty gon' buck?"

"Nah," he lied. No way was Richie Rich going out without a fight. A gun fight at that. "Come on."

Capo was still looking around like a tourist as they walked over to the next block. Bad Ass shook his head, hoping he didn't get them robbed. The satchel he carried looked like cash for a dope deal even though it only contained newspaper.

"Damn, shawty!" Capo protested when they stepped inside the tenement building. Bad Ass was in a zone and didn't even notice it. They paused on the landing for a quick briefing.

"Don't move 'til I move. When I buss, you buss," Bad Ass told his nodding partner in crime. Bad Ass knocked on the door, passing the unseen point of no return. This wasn't Bed-Stuy, but it was still do or die. He held his breath when he heard steps coming towards the door.

"Who?" Rich demanded as he unlocked the door.

"Me!" Bad Ass replied since he didn't want to announce his name at a murder scene.

"Sup, yo? Who dis?" Rich greeted warmly then switched up when he saw the strange face.

"My partner Capo," he replied, looking at the strange face on the sofa. His eyes fell down to her heavy breasts then her thick thighs. "Yo' sucka fo' love ass cousin at home breastfeeding!"

"Say word!" the host cracked up. "Anyway, let's get to it. I gotta make a run 'cross town.

"Bet. That's it right there?" he asked of the duffle bag on the loveseat. Still his eyes kept going to the pretty girl on the sofa. It was by design since that's why she was there.

"Yeah, yeah. I'll count the money later. You know I trust you, my nigga," he said quickly.

"You shouldn't," Bad Ass laughed and pulled his gun. Capo followed suit and pulled his.

"What the fuck, B?!" the pretty girl fussed as she popped up to her feet. The nervous Capo squeezed off a shot that sat her back down.

"The fuck?" Bad Ass asked, lowering his gun. He had planned to spare her but now she was staring off at whatever it is that dead people look at. The pause gave Rich the split second he needed to pull the gun from the small of his back.

"NIGGA!" he shouted and fired at Capo. Bad Ass ended the gun fight by shooting him in his temple.

"Grab the work!" Bad Ass told Capo as he rushed into the bedroom. He held his gun eye high just in case someone was in there. The room was empty so he began the search for the hundred keys the man often bragged about. "Lying ass nigga!" he fussed as his search came up empty. He found a couple rolls of cash containing a couple grand and pocketed them. Rich's diamond chain went around his neck while the matching bracelet went on his wrist. There was half a blunt in an ashtray so he popped it between his lips.

"You find it?" Capo grunted in pain when he returned.

"You hit?" he asked instead of answering while looking at the blood on his shirt.

"A little," he answered even though it was a yes or no question. He grunted again while hoisting the bag containing twenty-two pounds of coke and followed Bad Ass out of the apartment.

"Be easy," Bad Ass coached as they departed the double murder scene. They tried to appear casual as they walked briskly down the block and around the corner.

"I...um...ugh...I don't think...I'ma make it," Capo stated as they reached the car.

"You ain't," his partner agreed and shot him dead. Bad Ass grabbed the bag and tossed it in the backseat before getting in himself.

Bad Ass stopped twice for gas and to pee as he rushed back down south. They were almost out of dope so he needed to get this cooked and on the streets as soon as possible.

Chapter 17

"Where's Capo?" Self inquired when Bad Ass entered the Eastwyck apartment alone. He'd already heard about Rich's murder so he knew how that part had ended. The news report didn't mention any drugs, which meant he'd gotten them all.

"Rich shot him," he said truthfully. It allowed him to make eye contact when he said it since it really was true. It was only half of the story, but it was still true.

"That's fucked up," he mourned. Not for long, though, since they had work to do. Death was a part of this life and he was 'bout that life.

"I guess," he shrugged. He'd never completely forgiven the crew for jumping him. Tweek, Stewart and Tamir would get theirs one day, too. They could live for now since they moved coke from sun up to sun down. One day, their sun was gonna set and never come up again.

"Let's see...what...we got here!" Self said as they dumped the ten kilos on the table. "The fuck?"

"Look at this bullshit!" Bad Ass moaned at the ten neatly wrapped bricks of bullshit. "No wonder the nigga was tryna rush me! Talkin' 'bout he ain't gotta count the dough, he trust me!"

"Man, that nigga was gon' beat us," Self said, checking each brick. Only the one on top was real, just in case they had to test one. The rest were 2.2 pounds of all-purpose flour. "Lemme cook this one up so we can put it on the block."

"Glenwood was straight?" he asked, hoping it would be.

"Yeah," he replied to show his displeasure. "They need more but we ain't got shit to give 'em."

"Don't worry. I'ma find us a connect," Bad Ass sighed. He had no idea how, where, or when, but knew he had to.

****

"Why don't we just take what we have and leave? Let's just go," Angel pleaded. She and Capo had grown up together since preschool. His death had hit close to home since Self was supposed to have made that trip.

"We don't have enough. Just a few more flips and we'll be good," he replied.

If only Little Self had any idea how many men had made that exact same statement before dying or going to prison. It's always just one more flip or one more lick. Greed is a thirst that can never be quenched. It will never be enough.

"Look at this!" Angel insisted and hopped her fine ass off the bed. Her black ass checks were hanging out of the yellow panties had his full attention when she bent over into the closet. She came up with the tote bag that served as their savings account. She dumped it out on the bed. "Don't have enough! How much we need?!"

"Chill, ma!" he said as she frantically spread out the money. He had to wrap his arms around her to calm her down. "This ain't but a hundred grand. We need two or three times that much to set up shop.

Angel broke down in heavy sobs. Part of it was from the death that had hit so close to home. Part of it was frustration with life in the hood. Another part was that her mother had yet to come see her baby.

"Chill, ma, it's all good," Self comforted and held her tightly. He looked over to make sure the outburst didn't wake up their sleeping baby. He had planned to try to get a little before she awoke until Angel went on a tangent. He began to add soft kisses and caresses.

"Mmm," Angel moaned and squirmed like he hoped she would. She turned her face to meet his lips. Another moan escaped when he slipped his tongue in her mouth. She lay down, letting him know she was ready.

Angel lifted her hips to help him remove her panties. That's called an assist in basketball. She spread her legs wide in invitation. Self had to take a second to marvel at the pretty pussy. He slid a finger in and it came out glistening from her juices. When he pulled the puff of pubic hair apart, a pretty pink clit popped out like it dared to be licked. Self was never one to shy away from a dare so he leaned in and licked it.

"Ssss!" she hissed and arched her back, lifting off the bed. It was reactions like that that lead to dudes getting addicted to eating pussy.

Little Self licked the little clit, making his girl buck and writhe from pleasure. He didn't really know how to eat vagina so he followed her body. He went where it went and stopped where it stopped. They both found out that she was squirter when she came and it squirted in his face.

"Damn!" he exclaimed at his handiwork. He watched proudly as Angel made fuck faces from the intense orgasm. Once she came down, he made his plea. "My turn?"

"Oh, I guess!" she huffed and giggled. She certainly couldn't say no after that performance.

Angel kissed down Self's body as he shimmied out of his boxer shorts. Just below his belly button, she came face to face with his throbbing erection. She fondled it curiously for a minute than gave it a kiss. One kiss led to another until she parted her lips and took him inside her mouth.

Self had gotten plenty of head in his seventeen years but having the person he loved do it because she loved him was extra. Her mouth felt extra hot as it sucked him in extra tight, causing him to cum extra hard.

"Self!" Angel shrieked when she felt her mouth fill with a salty slime. She bolted from the bed and ran into the bathroom to spit. Meanwhile, Self used her saliva to get the rest out. She returned to find him still stroking himself to stay hard. "That's not funny!"

"I'm...not...laughing," he laughed and giggled at her reaction. She pouted but still propped herself up on her hands and knees. Self came around her and slid inside. The couple spent the rest of the night copulating.

****

"I don't buy that shit for one second, shawty," Tweek protested to Tamir in the trap. "How Cap get kilt and ol' boy ain't got a scratch on him?"

"And they talking 'bout they ain't get nothing but a brick!" Tamir replied. Had it come from Self, they may have gone for it but not Bad Ass. They didn't really like or trust the out of towner. They only tolerated him since he had the work.

"Now they tryna find a connect. I should put them on my cousin Yella," Tweek suggested.

"Yella? Yella Boy ain't got no work! He a jack boy," Tamir reminded. Tweek's cousin Yella Boy was one of the city's most notorious armed robbers.

"Exactly! Oh, here come that nigga now," he said as Bad Ass approached. Tweek sucked his teeth at his cocky swagger but was all smiles when he arrived. "My nigga Bad Ass!"

"Sup, yo," he replied giving them dap. "This shit poppin or what?"

"Yeah, shit booming. We getting some of that Glenwood traffic, too," Tamir replied. "Oh yeah, we may have a connect for you. Tweek cousin got some work."

"Say word!" Bad Ass cheered. "Set that shit up, B!"

****

"That fuck boy done cut us off now, huh?" Lil-C growled. He and Git stood in the trap without a single rock between them. That's the equivalent of not having a pot to piss in.

"Hell naw! All our junkies running over to Eastwyck to cop," Git replied. They took that to mean they were keeping all the work to themselves.

"And he fucking Kisha. I heard she pregnant," Lil-C added insult to his partner's injured feelings. Git had been trying to link back up with her but got nowhere. Not after denying their child. Now that the kid was dead, he came back around. It was some real Animal Planet type shit.

"So!" he shot back. "He won't be fucking her fo' long!"

Both men glared at Bad Ass' new used truck. The black Yukon sported twenty-four inch black rims and black tint. Bad Ass didn't even acknowledge them as he rushed to scoop up Kisha. It was rude even though he didn't mean to be. Kisha had been talking real dirty on the phone so he couldn't wait to get her into a hotel room to prove it.

"Go get them choppers!" Git demanded.

Chapter 18

Surveillance had been pulled from Cameisha since they now knew who she was, where she was and where she would be in a couple weeks. The six weeks for both mother and child was the perfect time to make the formal introductions. Good thing, too, because 'you know who' had come for a visit. Had he seen Josito and Carlos staking out his grandmother's house, there would have be a serious problem.

"Look who's here!" Diedra squealed when Killa walked in the door.

Everyone in the room winced as she wrapped him up in one of her grandma hugs. Even Trigga swore he could see for a split second when she caught him in one. They held their breath along with him and finally took a breath when she let him go.

"Hey, baby," Sincerity purred lustfully and got her a hug as well. This one was soft and sensual after the tight and violent one.

"Hey, yourself," he replied, sounding sexy. Cameisha giggled on the sofa for attention. "There goes my niece! What you got there?"

"My baby," she said proudly. She beamed brightly as he came over to inspect the child.

"Uh oh, dope boy and dope girl have a baby," he laughed. "I'm almost afraid to ask what you named him."

"Cameron Forrest-Jackson, thank you very much!" she replied.

"Rest in peace, cousin Cam," Killa said and lowered his head in sorrow. Then he cracked up laughing along with everyone else. Except for Trigga who wasn't in the know.

"What? What?" He turned towards the voices looking for an in on the joke.

"Anyway, look...what...I got you, Unc," Cameisha said as she pulled out his present. He extended his arm so she could secure the watch on his wrist.

"Aww, thanks. This is...nice!" he exclaimed at the gold diamond crusted Rolex.

"We all got one," Sincerity said, holding hers up. Trigga, Grandma and Sincerity's son Xavier all held theirs up as well.

"Poor child can't stop buying stuff," Grandma snitched. "She needs rehab!"

****

"You hear that?" Trigga asked needlessly. There was no way she didn't hear the thorough pounding Uncle Killa was giving Sincerity down the hall. The sounds of moans and skin slapping echoed in the otherwise quiet house.

"He must have really missed her," she chuckled. Trigga began rubbing his leg on her leg and growling. "I'm bleeding!"

"Not everywhere..." he said, trying his luck.

"Oh, okay!" Meisha huffed begrudgingly. She still wanted to go to the States after her six-week check-up so she gave in. Plus, she did enjoy pleasing her man.

"Okay, then," Trigga laughed when she skipped the foreplay and dipped below his waist. Usually she would kiss her way down, suck his nipples. Tonight, she dropped down and got to it. "Mmm."

"Mmm," she mocked as she worked her head. Only Cameisha could manage to be sarcastic with a mouthful of dick. She had no intentions of being down there all night and cheated. She wrapped her hand around his shaft and worked it with her mouth. Her pace increased when his legs began to shake and his breathing got shallow. Either he was dying or about to cum.

"Shit!" he gasped and exploded. Meisha kept right on going, driving him crazy.

"Mmm," she purred in contentment as her man moaned and shook in pleasure. She swallowed with a loud gulp and spat him out of her mouth. Her job was done so she went to the bathroom to brush her teeth. Trigga was snoring contently when she returned.

****

"Bad Ass! Come on, boo. Get up!" Kisha pleaded as she shook him.

"Mmph," he replied but didn't move. The combination of alcohol, weed and pussy had put him out like a light. Kisha had threatened to fuck the shit out of hm and kept her word. The only problem now was that she had to work in the morning. She wanted to get home to get cleaned up and dressed.

"I gotta go to work, baby," she whined. "It's already three o'clock."

"You going now? Thought you had to be there at eight?" he replied but still didn't move.

"No...but I do need to wash all this cum out me, off me and out my hair! How you gone skeet in my hair?" she pouted and popped his bare ass.

"My bad," he giggled like 'sorry, not sorry'. "Take my truck. Just come scoop me up when you get off."

"You sure?" she asked but he didn't reply. "Okay, then. Love you."

Bad Ass ignored the silly question about if he was sure. He wouldn't have said it if he wasn't sure. The words 'love you' snapped his eyes open wide. The simple words confused him deeply. He was too drunk to deal with it now so he closed his eyes again. A second later, they popped open once more.

****

"Here come that fuck nigga now," Git alerted when he saw the black Yukon. Lil-C responded by cocking a huge 7.62 round into the chamber of his assault rifle.

The deadly duo waited until the truck came by and came out of the shadows. They knew Kisha would be riding shotgun so they opened fire on the driver's side door. As expected, the driver mashed the gas and smashed out to avoid the slugs.

"Un-uh, fuck nigga!" Git vowed and chased the truck. He tugged repeatedly on the trigger until the gun clicked empty. He pulled open the door to get the last laugh but reeled when he saw Kisha inside.

****

"You must have really missed her," Grandma teased at breakfast. "At least we know whose coochie it is, cuz that girl was..."

"Grandma!" Sincerity shrieked, turning red from embarrassment. "The kids gonna hear you!"

"They sure heard you!" the old lady shot back and cracked up.

"Say something!" she demanded of Killa, who acted as if he didn't hear any of it.

"Yeah, pass the jelly, please," he said and kept right on eating. He'd planned to spend some quiet time with the family after the wild months with Yolo. He wished he could get her off his mind but the lunatic refused to go.

"Mmhm!" Sincerity spat at him figuratively.

"What?" he asked innocently. "I ain't said a word!"

"Yeah, but you sitting there with a goofy smile on your face! You must miss her! You must be ready to go..." was all he heard until he changed the station and tuned her out. All he saw was her mouth moving and neck rolling side to side. She was right, though. He did miss her.

Chapter 19

"Fuck!!!" Bad Ass shouted when his phone buzzed nonstop on the motel nightstand. He didn't want to be awakened but it was obvious that whoever was calling wasn't going to stop. He rolled over to the edge of the bed and snatched up the offending device. After violently pressing the answer tab, he demanded, "What?"

"You okay, B? Where you at?" Little Self inquired. His tone alerted Bad Ass that something was wrong.

"I'm good. Wh-what happened? You good?" he asked, sitting up straight.

"Yeah...uh...no. Your truck got shot up last night. Kisha...um..."

"She dead?" he asked as the world stopped while he waited for the answer.

"Nah, she's at Grady. Where you at?" he asked. Once Bad Ass figured out the name of the hotel, he relayed it to his partner. "I'm on my way."

Bad Ass got up and searched for his boxers. He found them on the other side of the room where Kisha had thrown them. After pulling them on, he slid into his jeans and boots. It took a few minutes of looking before he remembered his weed was in the truck. Luckily, Self had one burning for him when he pulled up.

"Good looking, B!" he exclaimed when Self passed the blunt. He took several pulls before asking, "What happened?"

"Don't know. Saw your whip on the news all shot the fuck up. I thought it was you until they said a female victim. Had wifey call around and found out it was Kisha."

"Man," he moaned and slipped into his thoughts. No words were uttered until they reached Grady Memorial Hospital.

"I'll be right here you," Self assured him.

They exchanged a pound and he rushed inside. "Kisha Redding!" he barked at the reception nurse. She was obviously used to it and didn't flinch.

"She had surgery this morning. Immediate family only and only ten minutes. She needs her rest," she said so soothingly that Bad Ass relaxed and thanked her. He made his way up to the room and paused for a minute.

Her last words came back and reverberated in his weed filled mind. There was no confusion now since he'd figured out what it meant. He knew because he felt he same. He still wasn't going to say it because he was way too thugged out for that.

"Damn, Kish," he moaned when he saw her laid up in the bed. Her eyes fluttered at the sound of his voice and opened. It was too much work to turn her head so she cut her eyes in that direction. "Sup, ma?"

"Hey, bae," she croaked, cleared her throat and tried again. It came out as harshly as the first time.

"Hey, ya-self. What's this I hear about you thuggin'?" he joked. He looked her up and down for injuries as he spoke. A large bandage covered the missing chunk of meat knock off by the AK-47. Other than that, she looked okay. She wasn't, though, but hadn't been told.

"You know how I get down," she laughed then winced from pain. She blinked a few times and stayed blinking as she fell back to sleep. Bad Ass watched her sleep for a few minutes before turning to leave. He met the attending doctor at the door.

"She gon' be alright?" Bad Ass asked hopefully. Half of the people he knew who got shot died, the other half were just fine. She wasn't dead, so she had to be okay.

"To a degree, yes," he said, giving a hint of the bad news to come. It was his experience that bad news was more palatable after a shot of good news. The good news was that she was alive. The bad news was, "She lost a lot of blood, which caused her to abort. There was a bullet lodged in her spine..."

Bad Ass tuned out after the word spine. He already knew what came next. His projects had plenty of wheelchair warriors rolling around them. What he didn't know was how blessed she was to just be paralyzed. If not for the metal door and the thick seat, the round would've torn her in half.

"Well, can she..." He paused to pick his words carefully. He was a thug but didn't want to sound crass. "I mean, does everything still work? Down there, between...um..."

"Wow! Um...yes. Yes, and no. she has no feeling below the waist, but her body could still respond to your touch. So she can have sex," he explained.

"Well, okay. What I meant was can she have kids. She lost one before and now this," Bad Ass explained his position.

The doctor's face softened upon hearing it. "She certainly can. A wheelchair won't stop her from being a good mom. She just won't be able to walk."

"That's okay," Bad Ass assured him. "I'll just carry her!"

****

"Where Bad Ass at?" Tamir asked when he and Tweek entered the Eastwyck apartment.

"At the hospital with...his girl," Self explained. He'd seen past all the tough talk and knew that his partner had feelings for the girl. "I got this."

Tamir twisted his lips at Tweek to show his dilemma. He actually liked Self and would hate to see something happen to him. Tweek shrugged his shoulders since didn't care, either. As much as he would like to see Bad Ass touched, he was in this for the money. The set up was for ten kilos at seventeen grand apiece. That meant they would split a hundred and seventy grand from the robbery.

"I need five mo'!" Miss Johnson blurted as she barged in. The woman was still a top saleswoman since she was in the trenches with the smokers.

Her twisted mouth twitched from a recent hit.

"A'ight, Ma, I...hold up," Little Self said, getting interrupted by a knock on the door.

"That's cuz," Tweek said and went to open the door. Yella Boy stepped inside, darting his eyes in every direction. "Sup, shawty."

"Sup," he replied, still scanning the room. He sat a bag large enough to contain ten kilos on the table with a thud. "Where that bread?"

"Right here," Self replied. He felt like something was fishy, but greed will make a person ignore warning signs. He needed this flip to make his escape out west. As soon as he opened the bag, Yella Boy sprang into action.

The armed robber didn't say a word as he whipped out a cheap nine millimeter pistol. It sounded just like the expensive ones did when it began to bark. A hundred and seventy grand splits a lot better two-ways than it does three, so Tamir was the first to go. A quick head shot cut him out the deal.

"No!!!" Mama shouted when Yella Boy turned the gun on her son-in-law. She rushed in front of him and took the two slugs meant for him. They both hit the floor from the impact.

"Let's bounce!" Tweek said but come to find out, a hundred and seventy grand splits even better one way than two.

"Sorry, cuz," the gunman said before gunning his kinfolk down. He grabbed the money and fled the quadruple murder scene.

Little Self lay motionless under his dead mother-in-law. He could feel her warm blood covering him. When it began to get cold, he slid from under her. Now it was back down to a triple homicide. Even though he knew better, he couldn't help but to check the bag Yella Boy had left. He already had plenty of phone books so he'd left the bag and fled the apartment.

****

"Mmhm," Kisha's mother huffed when Bad Ass entered her hospital room. She twisted her face up and glared at him so there would be no misunderstanding. She was not feeling him.

"Mama!" Kisha pleaded. "Don't start!"

"Don't start, my ass! And don't mama me! They shot his truck up tryna shoot him! Do he know you can't walk no mo'? Huh?"

"Yes, ma'am," Bad Ass said meekly. "I talked to the doctor. I got her," he replied and took Kish's hand on the opposite side of the bed.

"Oh, hell naw! I'm getting that check!" she shot back. "Greg already said he gon' shoot me something err week cuz he sorry."

Bad Ass pressed his lips together tightly to prevent himself from saying anything. Kisha squeezed his hand to keep his focus off her mother. He looked down at her but kept his ears on the woman. There was good information in her rant. Kisha couldn't say who shot her but her mother just had. The woman was still going on as she finally walked out and left them alone in the room.

"Who is Greg?" he asked as soon as the blabbering woman left. He could tell it was more than a one word answer when she started batting her lashes and wringing her hands.

"That's Git. He...um...he was my baby daddy, 'cept...he wouldn't claim her. I was a virgin 'til him and he acted like..." she barely got out.

"Did he shoot you?" was all Bad Ass wanted to know. That's who he assumed did it and he was going to murder him anyway as soon as things died down a little. Rock him to sleep like everything was cool.

"I didn't see but why else would he be sorry? And tryna give my mama money?" she asked, putting it together in her mind. Her mind flashed to the night of the shooting and she remembered the door being opened. "Yeah, it was him. He don't do nothing without Lil-C, either. Now I gotta see the dudes who paralyzed me err damn day!"

"No, you don't! You ain't going back there no more. I'on know what check your mom's beefing 'bout, but she can keep it. I..." he paused to check his vibrating phone. He enjoyed sending Self to voicemail just like he did him when he was with his girl. He began to continue but his phone rang again.

"Mmhm," Kisha hummed in jealousy. She twisted her lips and crossed her arms to make her point.

"Nah, it's Self!" he explained and took the call on speaker phone. "Sup, yo?"

"Yo, we got hit! Come to the spot!"

Chapter 20

"Hey babe, I'm gonna go check on my mama. She...um...ain't feeling good," Robert Ward told his wife.

"Mmhm," Sherry Ward hummed stoically. She had just spoken with the woman earlier and knew for a fact that she was fit as a fiddle. It made no sense to call him on the lie since they both knew where he was going. She may not know exactly the 'where' but she was perfectly clear on the 'why'.

Things had been going slowly downhill, sorta like an avalanche begins, since he'd fallen off the wagon. Neither spoke of his weekend away until his infected dick began to smell up the room. She suggested he see a doctor and he did. Of course, he came home and reported it was nothing after a shot of antibiotics. She didn't call him on that, either, but he wasn't getting anymore pussy. Not from her, anyway.

Robert fought the good fight but still lost. Every week he deposited less and less of his paycheck. Sherry had long ago learned to make do without his income. She'd managed to keep up the mortgage and the bills while he was in the trenches of drug abuse. He was just getting started again but was steadily building speed in his downward spiral, just like an avalanche destroying everything it came in contact with.

He may not have learned anything from the near death experience but she had. She added one more bill to the bills she paid all by herself. The policy only cost a few bucks a month since Robert was only in his mid-forties and still in great shape. If, or when, he died in the streets that he loved so much, at least she'd be able to pay off the house and have some money left over.

"Don't wait up. I may be late," he said on his way out.

She pressed her lips together to prevent the sarcastic statement from escaping. "Mmm," she replied to keep it inside. She then turned her face, giving her cheek instead, to avoid the kiss he'd offered to her mouth. As soon as his car disappeared, Sherry popped up and went upstairs.

Her side of the closet was full of nice clothes that she seldom got to wear because her husband didn't take her anywhere. That was okay since she'd decided to take herself out. She took a quick shower to freshen up and pulled on a lace bra and panty set.

"Hmph!" Sherry huffed at her sexy reflection in the full length mirror. She wore a similar set a month ago for her husband who acted as if she had on a potato sack. Even in her mid-forties and with two children she was still a very sexy woman. Her husband's neglect was a blow to her self-esteem. That's why she got cute and hit the streets.

****

"What the fuck happened?" Bad Ass asked as he and Self stood amongst the spectators at the crime scene. Luckily, Self had a change of clothes up in Angel's old room. He changed from the bloody ones and joined the crowd when police showed up.

"It was a set-up," he said as the first body bag was removed. Judging by its length, they figured it was the six foot, two inch Tweek. "As soon as I pulled out the dough, son started busting."

"Who?" Bad Ass wanted to know. "They got all the money? All of it?"

"Yeah," he whined in the same sorrowful tone as the question was asked. "It was Yella Boy. 'Posed to have been Tweek fam but he killed him, too. Killed Angel's mom, too."

"And got all our money?" Bad ass said since that mattered most. He didn't save and plan like Little Self did. Nope, he lived in and for the moment. He had a few grand at his hotel room residence but only because he hadn't had time to spend it yet.

"All of it," Self whined again because it mattered to him as well. He was still sitting on thirty or forty grand, but that wasn't enough to finance a new life. He needed that flip so he wouldn't flop.

"Who dat?" his partner asked when another black bag was carried out of the apartment and placed in the back of the coroner's van.

"Tamir, I guess? Yo, son was ruthless. He gunned us down like it wasn't nothing," he said, feeling like he was out of his league. Self had and would murder something, but this dude was a fucking monster.

"So am I," Bad Ass growled. Tweek had just gotten himself added to list the list along with Lil-C and Git. The technical term for that list is the obituary column.

****

The Chit Chat Lounge was a small jazz club off Candler Road in Decatur. It wasn't exactly swank but it was no dump, either. However, it did sit in front of a rundown trap hotel alongside I-20. The over forty crowd it catered to was just the vibe Sherry sought when she pulled into the parking lot.

As she approached the door, she could hear the cover band, Heart to Heart, doing a damn good rendition of a Cameo song. She happily paid the five-dollar cover charge so she could catch the song before it ended.

"Word up!" she sang happily along while winding her hips. Her shapely ass drew plenty of attention form the aging players inside. Her mid-thigh skirt showed off her thick thighs and panty lines.

Sherry clapped in gratitude when the band finished the song. She finally looked around the club for a place to sit and sip. Several mack granddaddies smiled, waved and lifted their glasses as her eyes scanned the room. The only thing worse than a player is an old player. She spotted an empty stool at the bar and made it her destination.

"Hey, pretty lady. Sup, sexy thang," two of the nimbler players asked as they flanked her. She only had one ass cheek down before getting rushed.

"I just want a quiet drink," she said almost apologetically. She held up her diamond encrusted wedding bands to prove it.

"Shit, I'm quiet!" one insisted since the other gave up.

"You can't be since I can still hear you," she said and spun the stool to face the stage and giving him her back.

"Bitch! Probably, a damn dyke," he mumbled as he slinked away.

"Seven and Seven," she ordered when the bartender got to her. She nodded and turned to fix her drink. Sherry and the lead singer locked eyes as he began his rendition of a Lionel Ritchie song. He had her feeling like she was 'Easy as A Sunday Morning'.

****

The Champion Motor Inn was a raggedy hotel that sat behind the Chit Chat Lounge. It had seen better days before crack took it into its death grip. Plenty of one-night stands originated inside of the club next door and were consummated here. Now they took their show to the hotel on the other side of the highway.

"I shol' hope Cray-Cray out here!" Nika exclaimed from the passenger's seat when Robert pulled into the Champion Inn.

Cray-Cray got his name the old fashion way; he'd earned it. He had a hair trigger temper and was known to whoop an addict. A couple had died but no one told. A couple more would die before someone did tell. He also had some fat dimes since he had an out of town connect. A new player was in town and was slowly gaining ground.

"Ooh, ooh! There he is!" she shouted like a white girl at a Beatles concert.

"We'll start with five," Robert said and pulled out fifty dollars he'd already separated from his other money.

"He should give me six for fifty! 'Specially after the way I sucked his dick earlier," she vowed. She was correct, good head does deserve a discount. A round of applause and twenty percent off.

"Sup, sup?" the shifty-eyed dealer demanded when Robert pulled up to where he was standing.

"Let us get six for fifty!" Nika demanded. She pulled the bills from Roberts hand and held them up.

"For you, okay," he said and made the sell. He gave her a round of applause as they drove away.

"Let me hold that while I get the room key," he said, reaching for the dope.

"Oh, you don't trust me?" she huffed and handed them over.

Robert refused to dignify the silly question with an answer. Of course he didn't trust her. He couldn't even trust himself and knew it. After all, his wife had held him down and he was still smoking and fucking. Hell no, he didn't trust her.

"Well, let's get this out the way first," Robert suggested once they got inside the musty room. He pulled his flaccid dick out and approached her. Sex would be out the question once they started smoking so he wanted to get off first.

Nika sat Indian style on the bed and opened her mouth wide. He dipped his dick inside and looked down to watch the show. Soon he was rock hard with her sucking and slurping loudly before.

"I wanna fuck!" he urged and pulled out of her throat.

"I'm on my cycle," she informed him. She still would if he wanted to but just wanted to give him a heads up first. "You can get some dookie love if you want."

"Nah," he declined and pushed back between her lips. He grabbed her head firmly and began sliding himself in and out of her hot mouth. Soon he was thrusting his hips and literally fucking her face.

The crackhead held on and took the oral pounding. Robert skeeted so hard she felt it hit her stomach. It was more than she could handle and escaped from the side of her mouth.

"Shit!" he exclaimed at the good nut. He was still rock hard and throbbing so he decided to take her up on her offer. "Turn over."

****

What the hell am I doing? Sherry wanted to know as she rode across the overpass with the lead singer. He pulled into the hotel's parking lot and rushed inside to get a room key.

The man had sang to her all night which was more attention than she'd gotten at home in a month. Between sets he would come over and verbally seduce her. She couldn't even remember what he said his name was or agreeing to come fuck him, but here she was.

"You ready?" he asked, opening the passenger's door.

She stuck her hand out as a reply and he helped her out. She gave up a generous crotch shot when she stuck her leg out to exit the car. He saw a wet spot seeping through the lace. Sherry was so excited that the friction from walking almost made her cum. A few more feet and she would've bust a nut in the hallway. She was far too turned on to play coy so she stripped as soon as they got inside.

"Shit, you fine, Sherry!" he exclaimed when she got down to the lace.

She could have said the same about him as he stripped naked, except she still couldn't recall his name.

Name or no name, Mister sure could eat some pussy. She was so delighted he chose to start with tasting between. She was almost embarrassed by how quickly and loudly she came. He sucked down the juices and kept right on munching.

"Oh!" she said, startled when he flipped around to put her in the sixty-nine position. She was faced with a dilemma when she came face-to-face with his dick.

On one hand, they'd just met so it couldn't be their anniversary. Hell, she couldn't even remember his name, so she definitely didn't know if it was his birthday or not. Those were some of the special occasions Robert would get head on. Then, on the other hand, it was pretty. He was eating her really well. She threw caution to the wind and opened her mouth.

"Mmm," he moaned when the hot mouth engulfed him. Sixty-nines are generally lopsided affairs. It's sometimes difficult to give and receive at the same time. They managed, though, and managed to cum at the same time.

Sherry's mind flashed to her husband as she swallowed the stranger's semen. She remembered not speaking to him for a while for not alerting her before ejaculating. She was so livid at the cum in her mouth that she was going to boycott him for twenty-four hours. Not tonight, though. Tonight she greedily gulped it down.

A condom came to mind as she watched whatever his name was insert his dick in her. He worked the head in and then slowly sank into her hot confines.

"Oh, boy!" he exclaimed. No way did he expect a mature woman to have such a tight vagina. His mind went to baseball, golf, needing a brake job, anything but the good, hot pussy and the pretty woman whimpering beneath him. It didn't work and he quickly snatched himself out of her.

Sherry leaned up to watch him ejaculate on her stomach. It was the birth control she and Robert used that resulted in their second child. She reached down and stroked his dick with her pussy juice. Once he stopped cumming, she put it back inside of her.

The man felt bad about cumming so quickly but made up for it. He caught his second wind and gave her the business. He fucked the woman face-to-face, then flipped her on her side. She felt him tapping on her cervix when he put her in the scissor position. He hit it doggy style, reverse cowgirl and scissor again, making her cum over and over.

"Shit!" he moaned and slowed his stroke. He was on the precipice as he slowly dragged his dick in and out. Out and in he went until he pushed against her cervix and exploded. And she didn't even know his name.

Chapter 21

"We're going to miss you!" Grandma Deidre said as she walked hand in hand through the airport with her grandson. Everyone had heard him and Sincerity saying their goodbyes all night long, so she had no problem hogging him.

"I'm...gonna...miss...you...too," he replied while scanning the airport. He had the strangest feeling that they were being watched or followed. Just like Spiderman had Spidey senses, he had Killa senses. Still, it made no sense way down here.

"Us, too!" Cameisha declared, holding up her baby while Trigga nodded in agreement by her side.

Grandma finally gave him up just before he boarded his flight. He gave Sincerity and the boys last minute hugs and kisses before heading back to the States.

"Well, I'm going shopping," Meisha proclaimed. "Anybody need anything? Anything?!"

"No, I'm good. Nah," the family all replied since she'd already purchased any and everything they could want. That money was driving her crazy to be spent. She had already run through close to a million dollars and still wasn't satisfied since she had no one to show off in front of. Trigga couldn't even see how tight her jeans were.

****

The day after Uncle Killa left, it was time for the six-week check-up for both mother and child. Trigga was happy about the blowjobs he'd been getting but he was ready to fuck his woman. They had a big, healthy baby and now he wanted some pussy.

"Right this way," a new nurse advised as she led the mom, dad and child into an examination room. Trigga frowned curiously because he didn't hear anymore voices. Usually, the office was buzzing with families but today, nothing.

"Right here, bae," Cameisha said, helping Trigga into a chair. She sat down beside him with their baby on her lap.

"I'll just take this handsome fellow for his test," the nurse sang softly as she reached for little Cameron.

"Um...okay," Meisha said, reluctantly giving up her child. This was her first visit with him so she didn't question why they were taking him.

"He's in good hands," she assured them. "Someone will be right with you, Cameisha."

"Okay," she replied and went back to shopping in her head. She had set her sights on a bad ass purse she just had to have.

Trigga frowned even deeper in thought and caught something odd. "Say, shawty, she called you Cameisha!" he announced.

"Nuh uh! Not unless she heard you say it?" she replied. She was so distracted by the purse that she'd miss it. They went back and forth about it until the door opened once more.

"What? Who is it?" Trigga asked in reaction to Cameisha's sudden silence. He'd clearly heard several people enter the room and could smell cologne.

"She doesn't know," a man replied. "Not yet, anyway, Tarvious."

"Wh- how you know my name? Who is you?" Trigga demanded and tried to stand.

"No, baby!" Meisha shouted. She had her sight and could see that two of the four men had machine pistols. The kind that could fire so many rounds in a second that it would cut a man in half. The men with the guns were scary. The man with the commercial food processor was even scarier, but the handsome man in the expensive suit was the scariest. "Where's my baby? Who are you?"

"People call me Sosa," the handsome man spoke. It was obvious that he was the one in charge of whatever was going on. "It's not my name, but it'll do."

"Well, Sosa, what do you want with us? Where is my baby? How much?" she asked, assuming that it was a kidnapping. She had millions in the bank and would gladly trade it all to get her child back.

"How much? Oh! You think I'm a common kidnapper, huh?" he laughed a dry, humorless laugh that sent a shiver through her bones.

"Look, shawty! I'on know what the fuck y'all on but..." Trigga said but shut up when he heard guns click and cock.

"OH, time for our demonstration," Sosa said happily when the door opened. In walked the nurse with a baby in her arms. Both parents could tell by its whimper that it wasn't their child.

The man with the food processor took the lid off before reaching for the baby. The nurse gave it a kiss on its fat cheeks before handing it over. He didn't even hesitate to drop it head first into the blender and put the top on.

"What! What's happening? What's going on?" Trigga pleaded to know when he heard Cameisha gasp in horror.

The man hit a button and pureed the child on the spot. Sosa had a sick smirk on his face as he watched Cameisha's reaction. He waited until the machine was turned off before resuming.

"Do I have your attention now?" he asked sarcastically.

"Yeah, man," she snarled. They had her down bad and it pissed her off. "That was unnecessary. A baby, yo?"

"The baby of a thief. Perhaps it would've grown up to steal from me, too. Just like his mama. Now his mama will eat that in a stew before I cut her head off," he explained in a tone used when giving directions to a lost tourist.

"A-yo, B, I'on even know you. I ain't stole shit from you," she replied, switching from a New York accent to a Mississippi one in mid-sentence.

"Sure you did," he replied happily then switched his tone as well. "When you killed the Salazar family, you stole my entire distribution network in America. Had you just killed Juan or a couple others, I would not have minded. Shit happens, but you wiped out my whole operation, costing me a ton of money! That baby's mother was my cleaning lady. She stole a watch from my nightstand."

"I'm sorry about Juan 'n' dem. I got money. I can pay you millions of dollars!" she pleaded. Now that she knew he was a petty monster, he frightened her even more.

"Millions? I lost BILLIONS, with a B," he boomed.

"I can't bring 'em back. I ain't no punk, either, so if you wanna kill me, go head. Leave him and my baby out of it," Meisha said valiantly.

"You don't understand how this works. You will be that last to die," he said, flicking pictures at her like he was dealing a hand of spades. In the pictures were her grandma, Sincerity and her sons. Then came pictures of Aqua, Samantha, and Jackie. "They all die first."

"So...what do you want?" she asked, wondering it could possibly be.

"I understand you are quite the dope girl. Small time with big time abilities. You will rebuild our cocaine network back in the States."

"I can't go back to America! The cops are after me for... Well, they're looking for me."

"No, they're not. You're dead so no one is looking for you. You will move in the shadows to establish my network. Once you do, you can keep your money and move on with your life."

"And how much do I get paid?" she asked greedily, causing Trigga to snap his head in her direction.

"Like I said, you get to move on with your life," he repeated. "I don't need nor want your money. I know you want to run over to the bank and take your money and run. My advice to you...DON'T!"

Sosa nodded to the nurse who rushed from the room. She returned a minute later with Cameisha's baby. She snatched him and looked him over for damage.

"Have a good week. You leave on Monday," Sosa said. He tipped his hat and exited the room with his security in tow.

"We...we gotta go," Trigga finally said after several minutes had passed. Neither wanted to breathe, speak or move until the violent men were gone.

Cameisha stood and led the way out of the office. They both paused when they saw or heard the office now full and busy, like normal. Once they reached the car, Cameisha headed straight for the bank.

"Wait here!" she ordered and bolted from the car. Cameisha took the marble steps by twos and rushed inside. She impatiently waited in line. Concepción spotted her and made a few adjustments to make sure she came to her station.

"Hello agai-"

"Yo, I need to withdraw a million U.S., or as much cash as allowed." Meisha demanded.

"You know we can't do that. What would Sosa say?" she asked. Cameisha was just about to hop the counter to kick her ass and take her money until a man walked up behind her. It was the chef who'd blended the baby.

"The bank president would like to speak with you," he said politely and turned around, knowing that she would follow.

She did. When they reached the manager's office, he opened the door and stepped aside.

"Come in, please!" the man behind the ornate desk called out and waved them in. "There is a hold on your funds."

"Why? It's my money!" she complained as her inner brat came out.

"I'm sorry. My hands are tied," was all he could say. If he didn't do what Sosa said, they would be tied, literally. Tied behind his back with weights tied to his ankles while he was dropped into the ocean. He didn't want that. No one wants that.

****

Plan C was dead as well when Cameisha came home to a flurry of activity. The cable company was running new lines to the house but she recognized one of the workers as one of the men from the clinic.

"This is what we needed!" Diedra clapped at the men installing the cable. The satellite was hit or miss down there so this was an upgrade.

"Yeah," Meisha said dryly. She knew full well that they would be watched as they watched TV. A deep sigh escaped her as she realized that she had no choice. She was about to be a dope girl once more.

Trigga and Cameisha were in a stoic mood the rest of the day. They'd decided not to tell anyone of what happened out of fear that they might do something to make things worse. After dinner, they retreated to their bedroom.

"Looks like you going home," Trigga sighed. There was no questioning that he'd need to stay behind with their son.

"Yup. That means I was swallowing for nothing!" she huffed.

"It wasn't fo' nothing! He-he-he," he giggled.

"He-he-he," she mocked then kissed her way down his body. This time, she swallowed because she wanted to.

Chapter 22

Angel rocked on the front pew of the funeral home like a person off their meds. She was getting worse by the day, making Self wonder if she didn't need to be on meds. Her initial reaction to the news of her mother's death was stoic at best. She simply said, 'Okay,' and went to bed.

"It's okay, Ma," Self said softly with their daughter in his arms.

It took a second for the words to register and she stopped rocking. She turned her face slowly with perplexed look upon it. "How?" she asked painfully. "She dead. How is it going to be okay?"

"Chill, yo," he urged when her voice went up. Even the rented preacher looked up from his script.

"I'm next, you know. I'll be the next woman of my family laying in a box," she nodded. Her alcoholic grandmother had staggered out into Candler Road's busy traffic and died when Angel was five.

"No, you won't. I got you, babe, just chill," Self assured her.

"Got me how? I'm still in the same place that took my mama and my grandma. Watch, one day I'ma be hooked on something, too! I'ma neglect my daughter, too! Then...then she gonna get teased at school cuz I got caught sucking dick all over the complex, fucking her little classmates for dope. I..."

"Chill yo!" he now demanded. No one else had bothered to show up for the funeral besides Bad Ass. He sat in the back brooding about getting some get back.

"NO!" she shouted and stood. She looked down at Self and into his soul. "You get me out of here. Save me! Save us! Get us outta here!"

Bad Ass looked up from his murderous thoughts to see his reply. He would never say it out loud, but he agreed with her.

"Okay," Self relented and stood. He pulled her in and let her cry on his shoulder. The heart wrenching wails even shut the preacher up. She lamented so loudly that even Bad Ass felt a tug on his own heart strings.

It was a funeral, so the few present assumed that the tears were for the dead. A few were but most were for herself. Her mother had never once come to see her child. Never once had she attended a PTA meeting. No birthday parties, cakes or bouncy houses had she given. Angel was getting her daughter out of there, one way or another. With or without Little Self.

****

"This is nice," Angel said, trying to show Self a house on her tablet as he drove away from the graveyard. He shot a glance at her instead of the screen and saw a happy smile on her face that was there despite just putting her mother in the ground a few minutes ago.

"Yeah, it is," he replied even though he didn't see it. He'd grown up in the crime, crack, murder, malt liquor, and food stamp infested projects. Anything was better than that. "How much?"

"Just one hundred and ten thousand dollars!" she cheered. She knew for a fact that he had it, she'd helped him count more than that to re-up with.

"Okay, reach in my pocket and grab a hun'ed out," he said sarcastically. "You say only like...like...it's only!

"Bae, I know we got that much. Plus, we got two cars, clothes, TVs, err thang we need. We can get jobs and..."

"Yo, we got about thirty grand. You forget it was a robbery and murder. That nigga tried to kill me, yo! Yo mama saved my life! It was me supposed to be in that box!"

"Well, I'm glad it's not," she replied evenly. He did everything for her while her mother did nothing. She was happy with the way things turned out. "I guess, we'll have to start with an apartment then we can save up for a house."

"We can't go nowhere with thirty grand! I need to get some work so I can come back up. The hell we gon' do in Houston with thirty grand?"

"What we gon' do here with it? It's the same if...wait. No, it's not. You gon' die or go to jail tryna get more money. Fuck some 'work', get a job!"

"Whatever," Self pouted. He certainly couldn't argue since she was right. Getting a job and being a law-abiding citizen scared him. It was strange, the unknown while he knew the streets.

"No, whatever is, I'm leaving. I'm taking my little money and getting on the road with my daughter."

"Our daughter, and you ain't taking her nowhere!" he corrected. Turns out, it was he who was incorrect.

"Watch me!"

****

"Hey, Sherry. It's me, Bill," Robert's boss greeted when Sherry took the call.

"Hello, Bill. How are you? Is everything okay?" she asked rhetorically. Her husband's boss would not be calling at eight pm if everything was okay. Her eyes involuntarily shot over to the drawer the life insurance policy was kept in.

"Yeah...no...um...well, you know I'm very fond of Robert, that's why I made sure I went to bat for him when...you know, his problem flared up. I made sure to hold his job while he went to rehab."

"You did. You were a wonderful friend to him, to us," she agreed.

"I...um...I can't help anymore. It's out of my hands now. We haven't seen him since midday on Friday when checks were issued."

"I see," she said without saying they did better than her because she hadn't seen him since he left that Friday morning.

"I can mail his last check, maybe you would get it before he did?" he offered hopefully.

There was a brief pause while she considered it. "No, let him pick it up," she decided. The bills were paid and she was afraid of him being broke and desperate. Besides, she had already taken him off the bank account.

"Again, I'm very sorry," he said, sounding sincere.

"Me too," she replied and clicked off. The conversation was pushed out of her thoughts instantly as that man came back to mind. "Ricky? Thomas? No. Mike?"

She still couldn't recall his name, but she remembered his thick, pretty lips moving when he introduced himself but missed most of what he'd said. Still, here it was days later and her vagina still buzzed from their night together. It ended the next morning when he lifted her leg and pushed his morning erection inside from the side.

"And you didn't even get his number!" she scolded herself.

****

Robert woke up naked and afraid in a rundown Dekalb County motel room. He looked around the dingy room for his dingy girlfriend but didn't see her. He popped up to panic but the door opened and she rushed inside. He could tell she'd copped some dope by the way she clutched her hand.

"Sup?" he asked hopefully. They had unofficially become a team. He would buy all the dope with his check until it ran out. Then she would turn tricks to pay until his next check came. Team work!

"I came up!" she cheered with fresh cum on her breath. She extended her palm to show the nice sized rock the dope boy paid her for an early morning blowjob. It was still decent after she chipped a piece off for herself. "You can go first."

He was too eager to get that glass pipe in his mouth to give a formal thanks. He did pass gas loudly to show his appreciation.

"Eww! What you been eating?" Nika laughed, fanning the air.

"You," he replied truthfully. He rocked in anticipation as she loaded the straight shooter. She put it to his lips and flicked the lighter.

The room filled with the sickly sizzle of the pipe as he pulled a steady stream of death into his life.

"Hell yeah!" Nika cheered, watching him take the huge hit. It was the equivalent to a three-point shot or long field goal in a crackhead's life.

"Mmhm!" he nodded and took sips of air to keep the drug in his lungs.

She joined him by placing another chip off the small block onto the pipe and putting the flame to it. Crackhead life. It can only end in crackhead death.

Chapter 23

"Somebody got some work," Bad Ass uttered as he crept by the apartments on Glenwood. He could clearly see drug traffic going in and out. A low growl escaped his chest when he saw Git and Lil-C serving customers. His hand reached and hit the turn signal without him telling it to. It would have pulled in and gunned them down, too, had he not stopped it.

Bad boys move in silence and violence, the late B.I.G rapped in his head. It was more than just a dope line, it was good advice to keep his ass out of prison, too. They were going to die, just not tonight.

Bad Ass busted a right on Columbia and took it all the way to I-20. He hopped on and back off at Candler Road. Even before he pulled into Eastwyck, he saw more drug activity. Young boys slinging rocks in the liquor store's parking lot meant they were short stopping the apartment complex. Someone had dope in Eastwyck, too. He pulled out his phone and called his partner.

"Sup, yo," Self answered. He was thankful that his phone rang so he could break off the debate with Angel. She was adamant about moving and had begun symbolically packing.

"Come to the spot. Meet me at the apartment," he said and hung up. No one knew the new-used car Bad Ass drove so he decided not to let them. He parked near the top of the complex and walked down to the trap.

"I ain't have shit to do with that shit!" Steward vowed with his hands raised. "That was Tweek's bullshit! See where it got him."

"We good, yo. Put yo' hands down," Bad Ass replied nonchalantly. "I see y'all back on?"

"My bad...we gotta eat, though," he apologized even though he had been slinging crack in this same spot since before Bad Ass and Self came down from scrambling for crumbs in New York.

"Nah, nah, you good! Shit, I need to get on, too! Who got it?"

"Um...a nigga called Cray-Cray. He pulled up and fronted us all an ounce. Said give him five hundred off it!" Steward replied. It was about twice what Self and Bad Ass paid them to sling rocks.

"Sho' nuff?" he pondered.

"Hell yeah! And he done hit up err' complex in Decatur. Shawty got some serious weight!"

"Hmp," Bad Ass replied. The conversation was cut short when he saw Self pull to a stop in front of the apartments. He gave Steward a pound and walked up to meet this partner.

****

"Five hundred! Shit, I'll stand my ass out there for that!" Self proclaimed when his partner filled him in. He let out a deep sigh of defeat. He was smart enough and man enough to know when his run was over. Why beat a dead horse and become a dead man or an inmate?

"You sounding like you giving up! I ain't! I found out where that nigga Yella Boy be at. He dead. Lil-C dead. Git dead. I'ma kill Steward then..."

"Go to prison forever. Son, it's over. I'm down for getting Yella cuz son tried to dead me. Maybe we can get our bread back, too, but this shit over, yo! My girl 'bout to bounce..."

"That's what this shit about, huh?" he dared. "Wifey done broke you down."

"B, it's over! How we supposed to compete with a nigga selling five-hundred-dollar ounces?"

"Sell yours for four-fiddy," a voice said from the kitchen. Self and Bad Ass looked at each other for an answer then both pulled their guns.

"Who dat?!" Bad Ass demanded as he crept forward. Meanwhile, Self kneeled into a shooter's stance ready to shoot.

"Y'all can't kill me, I'm already dead," Cameisha laughed as she came out the kitchen with her hands raised.

Self and Bad Ass blinked and stared as if they were trying to figure out who she was. Her skin was darker and her hair was lighter but she looked just like Cameisha. But that made no sense since Cameisha was dead. They'd attended her funeral.

"If you ain't gonna shoot, you need to put them thangs down and come give me a hug!" she insisted. No one smiled like Cameisha so when she did, they knew it was her. Both guns thudded to the floor as they rushed over to embrace their sister.

"How'd you..." Self asked as she squeezed him.

"It don't even matter. I'm here and we got work to do!" she replied. "Go kill who you need to kill and get ready. I got a boatload of coke on the way!"

****

"So there's hope," the doctor finished as Bad Ass walked into the room.

"Hope for what?" he asked. It was unnecessary, but he was always jealous of the handsome young doctor who attended to Kisha.

"For me to walk!" Kisha cheered at the good news. "I might walk again!"

"Might... IF the nerves heal and you have surgery. There's hope, but it's expensive."

"I'll pay for it. I'on care how much it cost!" Bad Ass declared. At the moment, he only had around ten grand to his name. He only had that because all of the bullshit that broke out before he had the chance to jack it off.

"Well...it's upwards of a hundred thousand. There are grants and charities that-"

"I said, I got it!" Bad Ass repeated, causing Kisha to cheese.

"Very well," the doctor nodded with a half-smile and left the room.

"Hey, baby," Kisha cooed once they were alone. She puckered up for the kiss she knew was coming.

"Hey yaself, Ma," he replied and kissed her lips. The happy moment only lasted for a moment before she sighed and twisted her lips ruefully. "What? What's wrong?"

"I get released today. I just hate going back to them 'partments," she moaned. "Hate having to deal with my mama. Hate having to see them niggas who did this to me!"

"You don't gotta deal with none of that shit! I told you, I got you. Fuck them clothes, I'll buy you new shit! Fuck yo' moms, she can keep that check she so worried about," he insisted. He left out the part about murdering Git and Lil-C the first chance he got, but she heard him.

"Okay, but I'm keeping my check!" she insisted.

****

"Hey, lady!" Angel sang when Bad Ass wheeled her inside the apartment. They actually attended the same high school but never spoke. They were never enemies, either, so the greeting was genuine. She didn't think twice when Little Self asked if she could stay with them for a while. As much as she hated to admit it, she respected Bad Ass for holding her down.

"Hey, yaself!" Kisha cheered. She was no punk but the warm greeting forced a tear to fall.

"Un uh! Ain't gon' be no crying! We got you. You family now!" Angel said, taking the chair from Bad Ass. She wheeled her into the room where she would be staying so she could show her all the stuff they'd gotten her. She was really crying then.

"So, what's up with that issue?" Self asked once he and Bad Ass reached the patio. He had to wait for his partner to light the blunt, inhale and hold before getting a reply.

"Mannnn, that nigga done tricked off all our dough! He riding around on 30" rims with a 30" platinum chain. Wearin' eight hundred dollar jeans, makin' it rain in the strip club," he replied, billowing smoke as he spoke.

"Fuck! Fuck it. If Meisha got that work like she say she got, we still good. Gonna pop this nigga top on the strength!"

"Guess, I gotta let you do the honors since he did try to murk you and all," Bad Ass said wistfully. Being a killer gives a person a thirst for blood like a vampire. And he was ready for a sip.

"Hell yeah!" And I got a new toy I wanna try out," Self said, rubbing his hands greedily. "Anyway, I'ma spend some time with my girls. I'll holla at you later."

"Bet. Wait! Yo, I um...good looking out, B," Bad Ass said. Never one for mushy moments, he turned and went inside.

****

"Here comes Uncle Bad As-...um, what should we call him?" Kisha laughed to the cooing baby when he walked in.

"Well, I know his real name but I ain't saying," Angel laughed.

"That's cuz my man is whipped and be talkin' too much! Ain't that right, Lil' Sammy?" he sang to the baby, making her kick her legs and laugh.

"Uh uh! Look at you. You gonna be a good daddy one day," Angel exclaimed. She didn't understand the awkward silence that followed but decided it was a good time to leave. "So, I'll see you guys a little later. I'll probably order out..."

"So..." Kisha said nervously. It still confused her why he'd stepped up to the plate the way he had. They'd just started fucking a month ago and here he was talking about the future and forever.

He would never tell her since he could never make it up. "So, now I'ma catch a nap. Gotta make some runs later," he said and helped her onto the bed.

"Okay, get you some sleep," she giggled and went for his zipper. She pulled him out of his pants and felt him get hard in her hand.

He had no complaints when she began stroking his erection. They turned face-to-face to share pecks and kisses.

"Shit!" he fussed when she pulled him to the point of no return. Good thing he'd planned to change because he skeeted all over his clothes.

Chapter 24

Aqua sat up in bed when she thought she heard the front door. She looked over at her son to make sure that he hadn't gotten up. Seeing him sound asleep, she smiled brightly.

"You don't have to tiptoe, Meisha! I ain't sleep!" she called down the hall to the intruder.

"Man! How you know it was me?" Cameisha pouted. She stomped the rest of the way down the hall and into the room until she saw Little Stevie sleeping soundly. "My bad."

"Girl, please! Once he sleep, only thing that can wake him up is morning," Aqua laughed. "Anyway, it had to be you. Samantha moved back home to have her daughter and I don't hear from Jackie."

"Damn," she sighed. Cameisha had been the glue that held the crew together. Without her, they broke to pieces and scattered.

"Self and Bad Ass be calling to check on us, though. Always asking if we need anything. We good, though, thanks to you," she said, knowing where the mysterious hundred-thousand-dollar check had come from. "Why you here?"

"It's a long story," she replied. She kicked off her shoes and climbed in the bed. Once they were comfortable, she filled her in. Somewhere along the tale, they both fell asleep.

****

"Be careful, baby," both Angel and Kisha said in separate rooms as their men got dressed. It was obvious from the all black clothes they donned and their bleak expressions that it was a serious outing.

"No doubt," Self replied as he pulled the black plastic case from the closet. He transferred an AR-15 from the case to a tote bag then turned to leave.

"No doubt," Bad Ass nodded as he finished dressing. He felt her staring and turned. "What?"

"You know you can still do it, right? I mean, I can have sex," she informed him.

"Yeah, I know. It's no hurry, though. Once you get that operation, you gonna be able to throw it back like you used to."

Kisha giggled shyly at the remark. Bad Ass came over and planted a kiss on her lips before leaving the room.

"You rea- Never mind," he said, stopping himself from asking Self if he was ready when he saw the bag containing the gun. That and the no nonsense look on his face said that he was more than ready.

Angel had given him a month to make something happen. If Meisha had the connect she said she had, then he could make a couple hundred grand in that short time. Part of him wanted to stay and see just how far they could go but the smart part said to take the money and run.

****

Sherry had no plans on having sexual relations again, however, she still showered and dressed in matching panties and bra. Cute but not lace since that's what had gotten her in trouble last time. No skirt, either, so she selected a pair of jeans and blouse. Heels put too much sway in her hips so she went with a pair of flats.

"Mmm, where should I go?" she mused aloud. Good thing she was alone because she was the only person she could have fooled. Anyone else would know she was headed back to Chit Chat Lounge to see whatever his name was.

Even her car seemed to know and automatically steered itself in that direction. Her lonely vagina began to throb as she got close. She got embarrassingly wet when she pulled into the lot of the club.

Ironically, her husband wasn't far off. He came down that very same street a minute later. He drove right by the Chit Chat Lounge and pulled into the crack infested motel. Armed with his last paycheck, he and Nika got a room and got their fuck on. Oral, anal and vaginal until they were both spent. Now, it was time to smoke. The avalanche was nearing the village at the bottom of the hill. The crash would not be pretty.

Sherry could hear 'what's his name' wailing away onstage when she reached the door. That spread a smile on her face as she paid the fee and walked in. She thought it would be a nice surprise for him for her to watch from the shadows and spring herself on him at the end of the night. The table furthest from the stage was empty since it sat furthest from the stage. She slid into the chair and ordered a vodka and cranberry.

Her favorite singer seemed to be singing only to a woman half her age sitting front and center. The young lady stared up at him with a wide groupie smile stretching her pretty face. Sherry was not concerned.

"Hmp!" she huffed confidently to herself. After what they shared last week, he would forget all about the pretty young thing as soon as he saw her.

****

"Uh-uh-uh-uh! Make it rain! Uh-uh-uh!" Yella Boy chanted and flicked bills at the booty clapping in front of him. Bad Ass shook his head at watching his hard earned money floating in the air. Not that he could really blame him, since he could hear her ass cheeks clapping together from where he sat.

"What up" Self texted from the parking lot. Yella Boy knew what he looked like since he'd robbed him, so he had to stay outside. The goon actually thought he'd killed all four people in the apartment. The news had reported that two men and one woman had died in a robbery gone wrong. Two plus one equaled four to his dumb ass.

"He in here" Bad Ass texted back. It looked like he might be a while so he ordered a drink and table dance of his own.

The waitress brought him his drink just as a young stripper came up to his table. She looked to be around eighteen just like he and Self. Her big yellow titties stood firm and proud above her hard stomach. A trail of soft brown hair ran down her stomach and into her bikini bottom.

"Um, hello?" the girl sang as she waved at Bad Ass, who was staring at her crotch.

"Yo, what up, ma," he smiled up at her. He couldn't help but notice how pretty she was in the face.

"Ten dollars a song. Twenty bucks for me to take my bottom... Oh!" she giggled as he shoved a fifty at her. She stepped out of the bikini bottom and displayed a plump shaved vagina.

"Turn around and bust it open," he ordered. He alternated his glance between his target and her vagina. He couldn't help but reach out and touch it.

"Mm," the girl moaned and leaked her wetness all over his fingers. She would've came on them if Bad Ass didn't have to go.

The stripper with Yella Boy was leaning over, nodding and smiling at whatever he was saying I her ear. He was negotiating and once the agreed upon price was met, they stood to leave.

"Aww!" Bad Ass' stripper whined when the stimulation stopped. Stripping wasn't just about the money for the girl. She was a stone cold freak and enjoyed the constant sex it led to as well. It wasn't uncommon for her to eat a vagina and lick a dick in the same day. Or at the same time.

"I gotta bounce, yo," he apologized with another twenty. She shrugged and took the bill, watching him text as he departed.

"On the way" he typed as he marched out behind Yella Boy. He looked down and saw his erection poking out in his pants. He pushed it aside and kept marching.

"Mmhm," Self snarled when he got visual confirmation. Looking at the person who'd tried to kill him was surreal. That dude had tried to off him, now he would return the favor.

"See what he spent our dough on!" Bad Ass said, joining Self in the car. They both watched as Yella and the stripper sat in an old school Impala lying flat on the pavement. He hit some switches and the car bounced up from the airbags.

"First chance we get, B," Self said as they pulled out of the busy parking lot. They could hit him in his projects but a dark street would be better.

"I got him," he growled as he trailed from a distance. They both saw the stripper's head drop out of sight. The Impala swerved slightly when she put her mouth on his dick.

"Red light coming up," Self announced as if his partner didn't see it. They both scanned the area for police and witnesses. Seeing none present, time slowed to a crawl.

Bad Ass watched in slow motion as Self leapt from the car. He then ran around to the front and jumped on the hood. Yella Boy looked up just in time to see the gun bark and spit at him. The top of his skull came off and landed in the backseat when the 2.23 rounds tore through his face. The girl didn't know how blessed she was that Self did the hit instead of Bad Ass. The latter would have sprayed her, too. The former spared her. He put two more rounds in his chest, just in case he could live without a brain, then ran back to the car.

"He dead?" Bad Ass asked as he swung a U-turn. Self gave him a 'yeah right' look in response. They busted a few lefts and rights until they reach I-20 going East. They then got off on Candler Road and pulled into Eastwyck. Self got out at the apartment and Bad Ass drove down to the trap.

"Sup, shawty," Steward asked cheerfully. He was in a great mood since the trap was once again booming. Not to mention, they had work and the New Yorkers didn't.

"Err thing cool," Bad Ass smiled and handed him his keys. "Thanks for letting me use your car."

"No problem, my nigga. You put gas in it?" he frowned.

"Of course!" he exclaimed. "Say, when you gonna put me on yo' people? I need to trap a little myself."

"Be easy, shawty," Steward said, enjoying having the upper hand. He had no idea how badly Bad Ass wanted to send him to the upper room. "He coming through tomorrow to collect and drop off. I'll see... IF I can put you on."

"Thank you, man! Thank you," Bad Ass said so fraudulently that he should have known that he was going to kill him.

Chapter 25

Sherry was buzzing from the vodka and sexual excitement by the time the band wrapped up its final song. Morris Day may or may not have approved of their cover of his hit song. Several hook-ups would now be consummated in nearby hotels as temporary couples left hand in hand.

The lights came on in case anyone didn't understand that the club was closing. It was the proverbial 'you don't have to go home, but you gotta get out of here'. Sherry was one of the last to leave because the young girl was still fawning over her boo. She decided to wait outside since she'd parked right next to him.

"Give it up, Lil' Miss Thang!" Sherry said when the singer left arm in arm with the girl. She was closer to shy than bold but had to take a stand. After all, she'd let him put his penis in her mouth and hadn't even known his name. Still didn't.

"Hello," she sang as he and the girl approached his car. He almost looked startled when he saw who it was.

"Hey, Cheryl! You got away without giving me your number," he said with a demeanor in between happy to see her and feeling put on the spot.

"Well," she began since he'd left without giving her his name. "You can certainly get it tonight. Tell your little friend to run along and..."

"Run along?" the young lady huffed. "You and your groupies, Daddy!"

"Daddy? Child, he is old enough to be your daddy! Now, run along so grown folks can talk," Sherry so sassily that she surprised herself.

"Um... I am her daddy, Cheryl. This is my daughter, Shanice," he introduced, obviously uncomfortable.

"Um...I...umm... I..." she stammered from embarrassment. Good thing her complexion was brown, so the chagrin didn't show on her cheeks. No words would come so she hopped in her car and took off. "How could I be so stupid?!" she fussed as she sped towards her house.

She pounded the steering wheel until her hand ached. "Made a damn fool of myself, and my name...is...not Cheryl!"

Sherry was blessed to make it home without getting into a wreck or being pulled over by corrupt Dekalb County cops. A DUI would have cost her her job and a ton of money. She barreled up into her driveway and pounded the steering wheel again. When she got out, she was surprised to see the lounge singer pull in behind her.

"What do you want?" she shouted hotly. She was really mad at herself but took it out on him. She glanced over at his car and saw that it was empty since Shanice drove herself home.

"Well, I wanted to make sure that you got home safely, first and foremost," he explained. "That's how we ended up in a hotel last week. You were quite drunk. I'm glad what happened, happened but..."

"I don't even drink much!" she shouted in embarrassment. His first impression of her was that she was a drunk. A pretty, sophisticated, sexy drunk. "And my name is Sherry! Not Cheryl!"

"Well, you said Cheryl. You were slurring your words so..."

"Oh my God!" she cringed. "Look, I'm going through a really, really tough time. All of this...is not me! Thank you for seeing me home safely. Now let's both go back to our lives."

"No," he replied. "Last week was no fluke. I want to get to know you. Matter of fact, let's start over. Good evening, ma'am, my name is Clarence."

"Clarence!" she cheered happily and shook his outstretched hand. "I'm Sherry, pleased to meet you."

"Likewise. Can I buy you breakfast?" he offered.

"Yes, yes, you can," she nodded and followed him to his car. He opened then closed the car's door just like a gentleman. It was just what the lady needed.

****

"A-yo, B, can I ask you a question?" Self asked as he drove back to his apartment. Bad Ass knew it was some serious shit because had it been regular shit or bullshit, he would have just asked.

"Sure," he replied since there was no better time to be candid than after you've committed murder. Police were still on the scene of Yella Boy's murder, busy pointing at the several cameras that had captured the shooting. All they would give them was a masked man with a chopper. Oh, and Steward's car.

"Son, you really gonna wife up Kisha? You know you ain't gotta do it..."

"A-yo," he cut in, sounding perturbed. "Where would we be if Meisha ain't send fo' us?"

"On that project bench scrambling for money to smoke a blunt and split a hero," Self said, making it sound as bleak as it once was.

"Well, I ain't leaving shorty in no wheelchair in no raggedy ass apartments with her raggedy ass mammy," he shot back.

"Nuff said," Self agreed. He pulled up to the gated complex and entered the code. He made sure to make plenty of noise as he entered the apartment. Once they were in, they shared a pound and went into their separate rooms.

"Hey, baby," Angel said groggily as Self walked in. She lifted her head and looked towards the crib to make sure their baby was asleep.

"I ain't wake you, did I?" he asked, glad that she was awake.

"Un uh," she lied as she watched him strip out of his clothes. She eased her panties off just in case he wanted some. He did. Murder always made him horny.

Self climbed in bed next to her and then rolled on top of her. She spread her legs, giving him access. They shared kisses as he worked himself inside of her.

"Go slow," she purred in his ear once he was all the way inside.

He complied by taking excruciatingly slow strokes. Not many of them because the heat, tightness and soaked young pussy got the best of him. They were both lucky she was so vigilant about taking her pills because he came harder than ever before in life.

****

"What's wrong?" Kisha pouted, still pulling on Bad Ass' erection.

"Huh? Nothing," he replied. His mind was on money so the hand job hadn't registered.

"Look, bae," she smiled, showed off her wet fingers. She couldn't feel it but her vagina responded to being rubbed.

"What's that?" he asked since she now had his full attention.

"Pussy juice," she giggled. "Look at how wet it is!"

Bad Ass took her hand and put her fingers in his mouth. He reached between her legs and played in her puddle. She hissed and moaned when he began to suck a nipple. He climbed on top of her and sucked on the other nipple.

The couple kissed as he slid inside of her. It was just as good and wet as it had ever been. She couldn't throw it back but made up for it with vigorous kisses and back rubbing. It got good to him, so he tucked his face in her neck and slammed up and down. He tried to pull out when the inevitable time arrived but she wouldn't let him.

"Nuh uh," Kisha protested and grabbed his ass cheeks. She used all her strength to keep him inside of her. This was a battle that even the strongest of men would lose. He gave up and exploded inside of her. Unlike Angel, she wasn't on the pill.

****

"We need to get us a bomb to sell," Robert suggested. The way he was nickel and dime smoking, his money would be gone in days. He knew it was his last check, his well had run dry. That meant that he would either have to quit smoking and go home or do some hustling. He had no desire to stop smoking, so hustling it was.

"Mmhm," Nika agreed as she pulled on the pipe. Smoke seemed to come out of her ears from the huge hit she took.

"Let's go talk to Cray and see what he will give me for five hundred."

"Mmhm," she said again, still pulling as if the folks from Guinness Book of World Records were there. She set another record by holding the smoke for almost two minutes before blowing it out. "Let's go!"

Nika led the way to the dealer's room. They were surprised to see it cracked instead of locked tight. Robert peeked in and saw the dealer having sex doggy style with a local junkie. He had his pants at his ankles while standing behind her as she was kneeling on the bed. A large pistol dangled from his hand as he stroked.

"Wait!" Robert advised when Nika lifted her bony arm to knock. He would hate to be disturbed while delivering back shots himself so he waited patiently.

Cray-Cray bent his knees and really started thrusting up inside the rental vagina. He treated it the same way most people treated rental cars, slammed in and out of it. "Mmhm, mmhm!" Cray said, agreeing with the building orgasm. He made two final, hard thrusts and went stiff. "Mmmm."

Cray-Cray proved how just how crazy he was when he pulled his bare dick out of the junkie. After finding out he was HIV positive years ago while in prison, he saw no need for condoms now. The hooker turned around and used her mouth as a wash rag and licked him clean. He tucked his dick away just before a knock came on the door.

"Come in!" he shouted and lit up a menthol.

"Hey, Cray-Cray," Nika sang like they were best friends. Turning tricks together every now and then did not make them friends. "Hey, Peppa."

"Hey," Peppa replied. She collected her payment of crack and scurried off to go smoke.

"What y'all want?" the dealer demanded. He looked Robert up and down in approval. He knew he spent well and drove a nice car. He was a sophisticated junkie.

"I want a nice little package I can flip," he said as if it was one of his business deals at work.

"Sho' nuff?" Cray-Cray scrutinized. Smoking and selling don't mix, like two dicks don't. "Tell you what. I'ma give you an onion for five-hun'ed. Now, you can sell it and make two bands. You can sell half, smoke half, and buy more or you can smoke all the shit up. Either way, it's cool with me."

"Well, I do like to smoke, so the second option is most appealing," the deal maker said.

Both Nika and Cray looked at each other like, 'what did he just say?'

"Whatever, but if you can hustle, I'll start fronting you ounces and you just pay me," he offered.

"Marvelous!" he agreed. They two didn't know that word either.

"Whatever. Just don't play with my money," he warned.

Chapter 26

Now that she didn't have to be a dope girl anymore, Jackie threw herself into her studies. She'd decided that she wanted to be a doctor and went hard in that direction. They'd narrowly escaped with their lives so she was glad that it was over. She was glad that that life was in her rearview mirror despite all the money in her bank account from it. Imagine her surprise to walk out of class and see...

"Cameisha!" she shouted as if the dead girl wasn't one of Atlanta's most wanted when she was alive.

"Shhh!" she shushed and moved in for a hug. Halfway through the hug, she realized that it was one sided and pulled away. "What?"

"W-wh-what are you doing here? Why are you back?" she needed to know.

"Long story," Meisha replied on the verge of tears from the lukewarm reception.

Jackie caught it and softened. "I'm sorry. You just surprised me. Let's go eat, you can fill me in over lunch," she offered.

****

"Holy cow!" Jackie exclaimed halfway through Cameisha's story.

"That's only the half of it," she confused. "Somebody already moved in and took my spot. I need the whole city to move all this coke and I can't even get my own spots!"

"Well, what are you going to do?" Jackie asked, making it clear that she wasn't down with whatever it was.

Meisha nodded when it came through loud and clear. "Something. I gotta do something," she sighed. Her appetite vanished in an instant so she stood to leave. Jackie stood, too, and they embraced.

"I'm sorry, yo, I just... I'm in school. My man, I...,"

It's cool, yo. It's my problem. I'll handle it," she said and left to go handle it. Cameisha left the midtown restaurant and headed east to Decatur. She was supposed to be meeting Self and Bad Ass, but decided to take a spin around town to see for herself what was going on first. She had a scare on Glenwood when a police car pulled right beside her.

The officer stared at her for several seconds before cracking a flirtatious smile.

"Fuck the police," she giggled and turned. She slowed down when she neared the apartments that Self and Bad Ass had once set up shop in. It was still booming since Git and Lil-C had hooked up with Cray-Cray.

Cameisha was supposed to be dead and didn't want to be seen walking around alive. She could get away with it amongst strangers but she was too well known in Eastwyck. A large pair of shades and a hat hid her face as she sprinted from the car to the apartment.

"Yo! Get the fuck outta here!" she exclaimed, seeing Little Self holding his little girl. She rushed over and commandeered the baby.

"That's your Aunt Meisha I been telling you about," Self said, equally proud of them both. There would be no her if not for her.

"What's your name, Lil Mama?" Meisha sang to the smiling baby.

"Samantha," her father replied since the baby couldn't speak. She could smile, giggle blow bubbles and other cute baby shit but couldn't talk yet.

"Hey, Little Sammy," she sang, not knowing the child's father was once called that. "Where's Angel? And Miss 'twelve go fo' the fiddy'?"

"Angel is at the mall. I'm 'bout to run the baby over now," he answered since it was easier to say. "Um...Miss Johnson..."

Cameisha looked to see where he was pointing and saw the blood stain. She handed the baby back and said, "Go take her to her mother."

Self knew this was no place for a child so he quickly compiled. He'd only brought her there to meet his sister and that was done, so he took her over to the mall to her mother. He was back in a flash with Bad Ass in tow.

"Sup, Ma?" Bad Ass greeted with a hug. "What's good?"

"Shit, you tell me, my dude," she shot back.

They migrated around the kitchen table that had always served as their corporate boardroom.

"Yo, look at...this shit!" Bad Ass exclaimed as he produced the dope he'd gotten fronted from Cray-Cray. "What's this look like?"

"It looks like... It looks like my shit!" she replied as she examined the dope. She could tell from the size to weight ratio that it was whipped but, unlike most whipped dope, this was that glass. "Where did you get this from?"

"Chill, Ma," Bad Ass implored when she snatched him up by his collar.

"My bad. I...um...where did you get this from?" she repeated, minus the violence.

"From the dude, Cray-Cray. A real reckless hot boy. He trapping out that motel across the highway. He supplying half of the Dec with five-hundred-dollar ounces. That's..."

"Seventeen-five a brick. Plus, it's whipped. Somebody got a mean connect for dirt cheap," Meisha summed up.

"That's great! Shit, we can get in where we fit in and come up! I got thirty-four for two and..."

"And nothing! This is fucked up! How the fuck am I supposed to get a distribution network if the city is flooded?" she asked then answered. "Time to get on that fuck shit! Whoever it is is in my way. They gotta go!"

"Say no more," Bad Ass agreed, ready to bust. "I'ma play this nigga Cray close to find out where he getting his work from. Son too stupid to be the connect."

"Do that. Look, it's just us on this," Cameisha said, straining to get it out. Jackie's snub had just set in but she knew her friend was right. This was her problem and she had to fix it.

****

Bad Ass hit the trap to sell the dope and keep tabs on Cray-Cray's operation. Niggas loved to brag and floss so he provided the weed and let the dope boys give up all the information they knew.

"I heard it's a new nigga in town who got all the work," Steward announced without being asked. Not to be outdone with new news, the others chimed in on what they'd heard. Ninety-nine percent of it was bullshit but that lone percent would be golden. Sorta like how the devil takes one truth and adds ninety-nine lies.

"They said shawty own every night club in the city!" Turk added.

"They said he owns the Hawks and....the Falcons" Q lied. He hadn't heard shit but didn't want to be left out.

"Word?" Bad Ass smiled and lit another blunt. He kept them coming and they kept talking.

****

"Girl... this fierce!" Angel shouted at her reflection in the mirror. "Chile, you the bomb.com!"

"Thank you," Kisha replied, proud and humbled at the same time. "I went to school for hair. Got my license and everything!"

"See, that's what I wanted to do," she pouted then decided not to give up on her dream. "I still am! I'ma open my own beauty salon, with a beauty supply and barbershop. Then I'ma put a restaurant next door..."

Kisha's smiled a soft, pensive smile as she listened to her new friend talk about her dreams. She had that same light in her eyes that people who make things happen happened to possess. No, these weren't dreams at all. They were plans.

"Well, I can teach you as much as you can learn before you guys go," she said, knowing the clock was ticking. She believed she was moving to Texas in less than a month, with or without her baby daddy.

"You know what?! You can come with us! You and Bad Ass..." Angel paused at hearing the words coming out of her mouth.

A few months ago, she wanted nothing more than to separate Self from Bad Ass as far as the East is from the West. However, for the week they'd been there, she'd seen a whole different side to him. It was nothing short of incredible how he cared for his injured woman.

"Hmp! I doubt that my man wants to go anywhere," Kisha sighed. She was down but Bad Ass was hood to his heart.

Chapter 27

"Hey, boo!" Cameisha cheered when Trigga answered his phone.

"I prefer Sosa," Sosa said in that sarcastic tone that made her wish the cat had nine lives so she could kill him over and over and over.

"Why are you there?' she growled. A chill ran up her spine as she pictured the smiling maniac with her family.

"I am not. We just tap in the line every now and then. You are very loud when you reach orgasm," he said, having overheard a bout of phone sex. Cameisha's face turned beet red from both anger and embarrassment. Sosa didn't get the reply he expected or any, for that matter, so went on. "We are weeks away from our first shipment. Have you found an outlet? We expect full payment in a week."

"A week is not enough time to distribute one thousand kilos!" she shot back. Not at the nickel and dime rate she could manage at the moment.

"It'll have to be. The next shipment comes a month later and it will be ten times as much. If not, I make a smoothie out of Little Cameron," he laughed and hung up.

Cameisha called right back but this time Trigga answered.

"Sup, shawty, you ready for our date night?" he asked with a smile on his face and dick in his hand.

"We gotta take a raincheck. What's it looking like down there?" she asked.

"The same," he replied since Sosa's people made their presence known daily. Grandma Diedra and Sincerity had no idea of the danger they were all in.

"Well, it's all good here. I got everything under control," she said, trying her best to sound confident.

"I know, bae," he replied sadly because he knew she didn't. They vowed their love then disconnected the call.

Cameisha had to step her plans up. Tonight was about to get real bloody.

****

"Give me a rock," Nika said, nudging Robert awake. She was the first to come out of the coma that had claimed them both after days of smoking and selling crack. Of course, she'd search the room for dope so she could smoke her back out before he woke up. Finding none, she woke him up to ask.

"Huh?" he asked as she sucked him awake. He was already erect from needing to relieve his malt liquor filled bladder but it was the thought that counted.

"I...said...give...me...a...rock," she repeated between slurps, sucks and licks.

"Oh, okay. Let me pee first," he replied and rolled off the bed. He stomped barefoot into the bathroom. After being burnt twice already by his companion, peeing was always the moment of truth. He was relieved to be able to relieve himself without the flames. Once he finished, he returned to her waiting mouth.

Nika was ready to get high so she threw her neck into overdrive. She sucked and tugged until she had a mouthful of cum. That should earn her a lungful of crack smoke.

"Now can I have a rock?" she asked, as salty as the semen she'd just swallowed.

"Ain't got none," he replied with a nonchalant shrug that pissed her off.

"Fuck you mean you ain't got none! All that shit you got from Cray! Don't be tryna play me!" she fumed.

"We had to sell enough to pay him. Now we can get some more. We'll have some to smoke and some to sell so we can get more," Robert explained.

"Whatever," she fussed, crossing her bony arms over her bony chest.

Robert shrugged again and got dressed. He missed his closetful of nice clothes as he pulled on a pair of Dollar Store jeans. What he didn't miss was being sober or his supportive wife. This was the life. Crack, beer and blowjobs.

Cray-Cray's door was partially cracked when Robert arrived. Another dope boy had just re-upped and rushed off to his trap to get some of that good weekend money.

"Sup, my nigga?" Cray demanded. He accepted the money Robert extended and counted it out. "How many I gave you?"

"Two. That's one hundred dollars," he replied.

"Oh, okay. Well, here's...there, since you doing good," the dealer said, handing him three ounces of the dope.

"Um...okay," he said, wondering if he was getting in over his head.

****

"You sure you don't want him to stay here and I go with you?" Bad Ass appealed. It wasn't like he didn't think Self couldn't handle it, he just wanted to bust his gun.

"Nah, I need you in the trap. You gotta get to this Cray-Cray nigga," Cameisha replied.

Self had a stoic expression on his face about what was to come. "You got us a bucket?" Self finally asked. They needed a disposable car to do their dirt in.

"Yup," Bad Ass replied with a laugh. "Steward was nice enough to let you use his."

"I don't know what that means, but okay," Meisha replied as the two howled with laughter.

"Nothing, but I'ma have to take him to re-up. So I can see dude again," Bad Ass said. He gave his brother and sister a pound and hug before departing.

"What's first?" Self asked as he and Cameisha headed out to Steward's car. He slung the bag of guns over his shoulder as they walked.

"Um..." she contemplated. They had a bunch of traps in apartments and motels to terrorize before the night was over. "Don't matter to me. Let's save the best for last."

****

Git and Lil-C got to live a little longer since Cameisha had decided to save them for last. Git got his last piece of ass while Lil-C got one last blowjob from a junkie. They met in the trap and smoked their last blunts and listened to Lil Wayne for the last time.

The Old English Inn was a decrepit motel near the end of Glenwood Road. Its close proximity to the highway made it a million-dollar trap. Cameisha was never able to lock it in before but now she was going to need to consolidate the whole city. The only problem with that was that someone else beat her to it.

"Shit booming, yo!" Little Self remarked as he and Cameisha watched the drug traffic flow by via foot, bike, and automobile. Neither would've been surprised to see a camel the way this trap was pumping.

"Welp, let me see what they working with," she sighed and got out. Her trusty bag lady costume allowed her to instantly blend into the bleak landscape. Most bag ladies didn't tote tech-nines in their bags, though.

"What you tryna get?" a young dope boy asked skeptically. A lot of junkies offer sexual favors for dope but he needed cash. A blowjob might fill their stomachs but wouldn't fill his.

"Let me see what them dimes looking like," she replied, rocking from foot to foot like an eager crackhead would do.

The boy didn't budge until she produced a ten-dollar bill. "Hmp!" he said, forcefully making the exchange. One look told her this was the same dope that Cray-Cray was pushing.

"Don't come out here no more. It's not safe. Tell whoever you getting dope from to fall back. This is my spot now," she informed him.

The kid frowned at the statement alone but really frowned when the gun came out.

Self saw his cue and got out with a chopper. Cameisha was nice to shoot at the kid's feet as he ran away.

Likewise, Self shot up cars and windows to keep loss of life at a minimum. Besides, who would sell the dope if they were all dead? A few dealers and junkies had been shot in the calf muscles and ass cheeks when it was all over. Over for them while the shooters moved on to the next spot.

Chapter 28

"I'm out!" Bad Ass cheered after selling his last rock. He was genuinely pleased to have made some dough but more so to go see the man they called Cray-Cray.

"I got...two more," Steward said. The words were still in the air when a customer came up and copped them. "Shit, where Self at with my car!"

"I'on know," came the lie. "I'll drive us over there."

Steward really didn't want to give up the connect but the trap was popping so he had to get some more dope ASAP. He let out a deep sigh at being removed as the middle man and agreed. "A'ight, shawty. We need to hurr' and get back," he relented.

Bad Ass made the short drive over I-20 and down into the run-down hotel. He paused upon seeing a cop car until he saw the door was open while a crackhead gave the cop some crack head. He loved this assignment cause it kept his balls empty and his pockets full.

"Room fifteen," Steward read from a reply text. Cray-Cray was crazy but smart enough to stay moving. He kept no less than five rooms rented at all times. Some to lay his dope, others to lay his guns, another to lay his money, and one to lay his head.

Bad Ass liked the feel of the gun tucked in his back. He entertained the thought of shooting Cray-Cray and ending it all now. Not knowing what Meisha would say prevented him for doing it.

"Come in!" Cray ordered in reply to the knock on the door. He squinted at Steward to try to recall how many ounces he'd fronted him. His mentor advised him not to write anything down so he handled distribution by memory. "Five, right?"

"Yeah, well, only three were mine," Steward replied, handing over fifteen hundred. He would have preferred to handle it by himself but Bad Ass wouldn't give him the money. "He got the rest."

"They call me Bad Ass," he replied instead of shooting him.

"Bad Ass, huh?" he chuckled. "Well, you good, money, so I'ma call you whatever you want me to!"

"Speaking of calling, let me get a number so I can get at you," Bad Ass said. He meant kill him but the dealer didn't catch it.

Steward watched his control vanish when Cray-Cray gave Bad Ass his number along with three ounces of crack. He received the same and they headed back to the trap.

****

"This car gotta be hot by now," Meisha suggested after they shot up their tenth trap spot.

"Been hot!" Self laughed. It started with a chuckle and built until he was cracking up.

"What?" she laughed, wanting in on the joke.

"We use dude car err time we gotta bust our guns. Dumb ass is gon' be linked to several bodies and don't even know it!"

"Ooh, y'all dirty!" she laughed.

"Nah, he might be down with that setup! Got all our dough and killed my baby's mom's mom," Self said hotly.

"You feeling that girl, huh? That's good. I like her, she's good for you," she asked, answered and stated.

"Yeah, once we get this money up, we bouncing out west. Bad Ass and his girl coming, too! We all gon' open a business together. Barbershop/beauty salon... We gon' call it 'Go On With Your Bad Ass Little Self'!"

"Kinda long and wack," Meisha laughed. It was short lived as she drifted inside her head. Her little brothers could end up dead or in jail. She didn't hear anything else he said until he repeated it.

"We're here. Git is dude in the Braves hat and Lil-C got the afro."

"Got 'em," she replied and hopped out and headed over to the men.

"This the last blunt," Git said, and prepared to light it. He meant out of the weed they had but Meisha was thinking more permanent.

"Look at this bitch," Lil-C laughed at Meisha as she approached. She did look odd with her face twisted into a mask of murder.

Cameisha had her hand in the bag gripping the machine pistol tightly. She tried to come up with some fly shit to say before gunning them down but nothing came to mind. She shrugged her shoulders and pulled the gun.

"What the..." were Lil-C's final words before the tech spun him like a top.

Git lifted his leg to run but got shot in his cheek and chest. Both men fell side by side and she stood over them and sprayed them with a three shot burst. The other dope boys in attendance were so shook by the sudden violence that they froze in their places.

"Now, there's a new player in town. Ain't nobody selling shit if they ain't selling shit for him! Don't make me come back!" she ordered.

The men and teens stood there blinking even after she was gone. They each turned to the other for someone to explain what the heck just happened. Cameisha and Self had made it back to Eastwyck before someone finally spoke up.

"I thought there was already a new player in town? Ain't this his dope?" one wanted to know.

"Don't know, don't care," another shrugged. He had to sling dope to eat. And since he had to eat to live, he planned to keep right on slinging, regardless of where it came from.

****

Self dropped Cameisha at her car and drove down the hill to the trap. Steward and Bad Ass we're almost done with the work they'd copped from Cray-Cray.

"Sup, yo?" Self said to his partner and tossed Steward his keys.

"Hope you put some gas in my shit!" he barked.

"At least!" Self shot back. He turned to leave to go home and heard Bad Ass coming behind him. Steward was happy to have less competition.

"Need to check on Kish," he said as if he needed an excuse.

"Mmhm," he said, accepting it. "Left ol' boy a present."

"Hope he enjoys it," Bad Ass cracked up. An hour later, Steward sold out and decided to go trick off a little of his profits. He opened the trunk to stash some cash and found his surprise.

"Oh shit!" he cheered happily as he picked up the AR-15. He didn't notice that it was a little heavier from the bodies on it. "Y'all dead. I'm keeping this!" Steward fondled the gun from stock to barrel. He pulled the clip and put it back. It had been wiped clean and now his prints were all over it.

"Is that...the car?" a cop asked his partner incredulously as Steward drove by.

"Nah." His partner shook his head. It sure looked like the same vehicle used in a string of shootings, though. The same car was also linked to a recent brutal murder. "Go on and light it up."

"Why not? Ain't nothing else happening," the bored cop said and hit the squad car's lights and camera, ready for action.

"Y'all late," Steward laughed at the blue lights. He'd gotten off all his dope so he wasn't worried about the stop. He had no qualms about pulling over. Both his license and registration were in hand when they approached.

"Let me get you to step out of the car," the first cop said nicely while the second played the rear with gun in hand. This is called good cop, bad cop.

"What I did, officer?" Steward demanded as he complied.

The cop cuffed his hands behind his back before responding. "For our safety," he said to explain the cuffs. (It's not legal anywhere except in every hood.)

Meanwhile, his partner began to illegally search the vehicle. "Jackpot!" cop number two cheered when he found the chopper. He was already cuffed up so they took him off to jail.

Chapter 29

Sherry rocked gently back and forth to the back shots Clarence dished out. His slow, gentle stroke made her cum over and over and over again. Judging by his rapid breathing and increased thrusting, she knew that he was nearing one himself. It occurred to her that he was inside of her raw, again. Over the last couple of weeks, he'd been skeeting in it like he owned it. She'd been meaning to say something about it. Who did he think he was, anyway?! Just cumming in her whenever he felt like...

"I'm cumming!" Clarence warned urgently, interrupting her internal fussing.

"Mmm," she replied and arched her back. She would have to say something next time. This time, she squeezed her hot vagina tightly around him to help him get it all out.

"Shit!" he said as he fell over. "You are too good to be true."

"You are, too!" she said, falling on top of him and smothering him with kisses.

This was as happy as she'd been in years. It was so much more than great sex. They didn't call what they had a relationship, but that's exactly what it was. They went on movie and dinner dates. They walked in the park. Spent late nights on the phone. Exchanged flowers, cards and teddy bears. Not to mention, the sex was outrageous. Life was so good that she forgot all about her husband, until she heard the front door open.

"Oh shoot! My husband!" she exclaimed and jumped to her feet.

Clarence was right behind her and scrambled to get dressed. No one can ever find their drawers at a time like this. He was forced to pull his jeans on commando style. She wrapped a bathrobe around her and rushed down the stairs.

"Who are you? What are you doing in my hou- Robert?" she asked as she recognized her disheveled husband. He was such a mess that he looked blurry.

"I live here. See you forgot that thought!" he said hotly. "I just came for my laptop and watch."

Nika had smoked and swiped so much dope out of the last package that he needed to pawn a few things to make up the difference.

"All of your things are in the garage," she said indignantly. He'd left his home and wife and now all he wanted was his computer. She wanted to argue so she could make her point, but he rushed into the garage.

Robert rambled through his own possessions like a thief. Fuck all the gifts and sentimental shit, he was looking for things to pawn. Once he'd collected enough, he went back into the house and tossed his keys at her feet.

"Tell that dude to pay the mortgage!" he fussed and stormed off.

Sherry stood there scratching her head in confusion. She'd been paying the mortgage and everything else since he'd decided he wanted to be a crackhead.

"Husband?" Clarence wanted to know when she returned. He was now fully dressed, waiting and expecting to have to fight the man.

"He was. He has a drug problem. He left me," she explained. That was the first time she'd said it aloud and hearing it broke her heart.

"Damn fool," he commented and embraced her.

The comforting hug finally allowed her to break down and get it all out. She cussed, screamed, wailed and moaned. Her knees gave out and the strong man held her up. It took ten minutes for her to release all the pain from all the years of neglect.

"I'm okay," she finally said as she pulled away, lifted her chin and wiped away the last of the tears that she would ever shed on behalf of Robert Ward. She'd finally run out of love. "Oh, but I do need to speak with you about your...ejaculating in me."

"You want me to stop?" he asked sadly.

"Actually, I want you to do it again...now!" she replied.

****

"What's wrong with you?" Nika asked as Robert drove angrily through a stop sign. He was so hot about his wife that he didn't see it until he was halfway through it. It don't count unless you wreck or get a ticket, so he just shrugged it off.

He should've been mad at her for fucking up Cray-Cray's money, again. It was a battle to sell enough dope to pay him before she smoked it all up. They were both getting tired of fussing with one another over dope. He was seriously thinking about trading her for one of the other crack whores in and around the motel. It was cool since she was plotting and planning as well.

Nika had to wait in the car while Robert went inside the pawn shop. The sticky fingered girl had been banned from most of the stores east of Atlanta. She was so good that had taken video replay to catch her in action.

Robert was still in his feelings about his wife moving on. In his mind, it was she who was in the wrong.

"What you got there?" the clerk asked when Robert reached the counter.

"A Rolex, Sony VAIO and this chain," he said, laying it out on the counter.

The clerk picked up the watch and twisted his lips at it. He could tell in an instant that it was real but still decided to short him. "I can give you...about...fifty," he said, sounding disinterested

"Dollars?! This is a Presidential! It's worth thousands of dollars!" he insisted.

"You might wanna take it back then because in here, it's only worth fifty," he said, playing him like a crackhead. "I can go another fifty for the computer and a hundred on the chain."

Robert was mortified at the lowball offer, but the total would be enough to make up what he owed Cray-Cray and that was all that mattered. Once he paid, he could get more dope and that's what matter mattered most.

"Since it's just a pawn, I'll come back and claim it," Robert agreed. If he believed it, he was the only one.

"Um...yeah, okay," the man said and removed two hundred dollars from his pocket. Robert took the money and ran without waiting to fill out any paperwork. That was fine by him since he put the watch on his wrist, the chain around his neck and the laptop in his car.

****

"You scared me for a minute," Cray-Cray said when Robert came into the room. He'd seen him leave the hotel without paying him and thought he'd run off. It's a small world in general and even smaller for crackheads, so he figured they'd see each other again.

"No sir. I do great business," Robert assured him as he handed over the money. He watched with pride as the count came out exact. He didn't need to know all he had to do it get it.

"That's good, cuz I don't play 'bout my bread," he said, handing over three more ounces.

"Excuse me," he said for passing gas loudly at the sight of the pretty slabs of cocaine.

"Don't be, happens all the time," he replied.

"We straight?" Nika asked anxiously when Robert returned to the room. She could smell the dope in his pocket so she knew that he was.

"Kind of. Only got one this time. We'll need to sell half before we get started," he lied. He had no plans of letting her smoke him into a hole. "Let me get a little bit before we get started."

"Ass or head?" she asked, since he could get either. He could get anal or underarm if he wanted. As long as it ended with a pipe in her mouth, it was par for the course.

"Vagina," he clarified and began to undress. Nika snatched her shorts and panties off in one motion to beat him getting naked. Her beat up box required saliva to get him wet so she spat on her hand and slapped her floppy vagina lips.

He grabbed her ankles and lifted them up so high that her ass came off the bed. She guided him inside and took a pounding. He was mad about that car being parked in his driveway and took it out on her insides. It was good thing that her pussy was so dilapidated or it would have been painful. The lack of friction in her wall-less vagina frustrated him.

"Open," he ordered when he moved the party up to her mouth. She let him in and gagged with every stroke. Luckily, she could clamp down enough to get him off. He was so far down her throat that she didn't even have to swallow. He skeeted almost directly into her stomach.

"Now give me a rock!"

Chapter 30

"Yo, this shit is crazy!" Cameisha lamented. "I been busting at these niggas all week and they won't stop slinging!"

"They gon' starve to death if they do," Self reasoned. It made perfect sense but she was beyond reason. Time was almost up and she was no further than when she started.

Self and Bad Ass spent all day and all night in the trap. Self's clock was ticking, too, before his girl took their child and left. He was able to add ten more grand to their stash but it still wasn't enough. Bad Ass planned to let Kisha go with them while he got the money for her surgery. The trap was his Go-Fund Me.

"Look, we gonna have to put the press on this nigga Cray-Cray. Take me to him. I'ma make him an offer he can't refuse," she said in that 'get down or lay down' tone of voice.

"A'ight but I'on think that's gon' get us anywhere. We'll swing by the motel later on. Let me finish my pack first," Bad Ass said. He took her silence as a yes and hit the trap. Self was right behind him since Steward was busy fighting a murder and multiple aggravated assault charges.

"What sis got going?" Self asked. He had his own ideas but needed a second opinion.

"I'on know, bruh," he replied warily. "I mean, I'm down, no matter what. I just... I'on know."

****

"Shit!" Robert cussed when he woke up. He hadn't realized that he had even gone to sleep until he woke up alone. A scan of the room came up as empty as the bed.

"Nika?" he called into the bathroom. No reply came so he went in to confirm her absence. The toilet explained to him why he felt uncomfortable. He was already naked so he dangled his dick over the bowl. That's when the flames started. "Owweee! That bitch!"

After a painful piss, he stomped back into the room. He decided this was a good time to leave her. She could keep the room and a few rocks but it was time to move on. He checked his side of the bed for his pants but didn't find them.

"Hmp?" he asked, scratching his head when he didn't see them on the other side either. He dropped down and checked under the bed but came up empty again.

He knew in that second that she was gone but still tore the room up looking for her and/or the dope. He had just paid Cray-Cray and had received five more ounces. He retraced his steps and tried to put things together.

"Okay, we took a blast. She fixed me a drink, I..." he said, getting stuck there. "She drugged me!"

He was one hundred percent correct. She'd literally drugged him so she could drag him figuratively. The second he passed out, she got to work. He'd planned to leave her a few rocks when he left her but she didn't leave him shit. Not only did she take every crumb of dope, she took his clothes and car as well. She didn't even leave the pipe full of residue behind.

"Shit!" he said and flopped down on the bed. "I'll just go inform him of what happened."

Robert was from a world where honesty was the best policy. A reasonable place where reasonable people could reason with each other. He should have stayed there because this was a different world. He solved his clothing dilemma by wrapping a sheet around himself. It was dark now so he wouldn't draw too much attention. He opened the room's door and checked both ways as if crossing the street.

"You working?" a man called from his car when he saw Robert wearing nothing but a sheet. Robert lifted his head in indignation at being mistaken for one of the many gay prostitutes in the area. He really couldn't get mad, though, since he was wearing a sheet.

"Come in!" Cray-Cray barked in response to the knock on his door. He was in a foul mood upon hearing about two more run-offs. His mentor told him not to sweat it because it was part of the game. He took it as a weakness and got angry.

"Excuse me. We have a little situation," Robert began.

Cray-Cray frowned up at him wearing a sheet and got even angrier. "Is you trying me?" he growled and cocked his head. "We ain't in prison! I don't fuck around!"

"Huh? I... Oh no! It's just that my companion ran off with my clothes," he chuckled. "Took my car, clothes and unfortunately, all of the product I got from you."

"So, you ain't got my money?" he dared. "Shawty, do not tell me you ain't got my bread?"

"Well, I don't, but..." would be Robert Ward's final words.

Cray-Cray closed the distance in a blur. He hit him with a blow that knocked him out before he hit the ground. The first stomp woke him back up, but the next one put him back to sleep. The rest went from fatal to futile as it went on long after he'd passed on.

"Yeah!" Cray snapped at the knock on the door. He was still open for business so he yelled, "Come in!"

"Sup, yo, I ..." Bad Ass greeted until he saw the corpse. Cray-Cray's expensive jeans were covered in blood up to the knees like he had been wading in it.

"Bitch ain't have my money," he explained. "Who you got with you?"

"Huh? Oh, yo, this my sister, um..." he said, searching for a fake name.

"Cameisha," Cameisha said. She could already tell how this was going to end and saw no reason not to use her real name. The person he would be able to tell was dude laying on the floor.

"Sup, Cameisha?" he greeted, licking his lips and grabbing his crotch. He lived in a world where that and a dime of crack would get him laid. Fucking with her was about to get him laid out.

"Bruh, I'm here on business," she said, barely keeping her composure.

"I hear you moving major work. I need you on my team. I'll pay you double whatever you getting now."

"Bitch, I'm straight! I'm the man next to the gotdamn man!" he shot back. He wasn't, though, because the man had men like him in every county of Metro Atlanta. He could and would be replaced in a second. "This nigga got long bread! Own Club Illusions and err thang. Now, hop in that sack and let a nigga drop some dick in ya."

"Are you sure?" Meisha sighed at Plan A slipping away.

"I'm sure I'll fuck the shit outta you!" he laughed and looked to Bad Ass to laugh along with him.

"Plan B," she shrugged. Bad Ass reached in his back and snatched his pistol.

Cray-Cray's eyes went wide at the sight of the gun just before getting shot right between them. His knees buckled and down he went, right next to Robert. Bad Ass rushed around the room and collected almost a quarter kilo of cooked coke. Cameisha was already at the car by the time he caught up.

"Yo, I'm trying to clear all that coke off the street!" she complained. "My shit will be here in days and..."

"And we'll be done already! Ma, we gotta eat," he pleaded

She knew he was right but still sighed loudly. "So, now what? We hitting up Club Illusions?"

"Not we. Me!" she replied. "Guess I need to go shopping."

Chapter 31

"I knew it! I fuckin' knew it," Big Shawn swore, pointing his finger in Cameisha's face. "When I heard about the bomb at the funeral, I knew it was Sampson, but I knew it wasn't you!"

"Are you going to let me in?" she asked curtly. It hurt her feeling that everyone didn't fall for her ruse.

"Yeah, yeah, come on in. What can I do for you? How's your uncle?" Big Shawn rambled happily.

"He fine, I guess," she guessed. "I need a burner."

"What, a tank? A bazooka?" he quipped.

"Nah, something compact. Something I can conceal," she replied and followed him into the showroom.

He stopped at a table full of pistols and plucked up one. "Something like this?" he asked, holding up a bite-sized forty caliber. "It'll fit in a purse but make a nigga turn a full flip when you hit him.

"Too big," she said, looking at the gun in her palm. "Won't fit,"

"Where you tryna hide it?" he asked causing her eyes to flutter sheepishly. "Oooh. Okay. Um...how's this? Thirty-two caliber, two shots."

"This should get it," she said of the small pistol. Now it was her turn to embarrass him. "Hold up, let me see if it fits..."

"Whoa!" he said, raising his hands to stop her from pulling her jeans off.

"Okay, this is cool. What I owe you?" she asked.

"Depends on who you gonna use it on. If it's some piece of shit, it's free," he offered and loaded two bullets in the gun.

"The owner of Club Illusions. He in my way," she replied and noticed him cringe. "What, you know him?"

"Um...nah. Hold up. Let me upgrade you to magnum bullets," he said and swapped out the bullets. "You don't owe me nothing. Just tell dude I said hello when you bust him."

"Copy that," she said and set off to shop for her night out.

****

"Boss! Our boy out in Decatur got hit," Convict said excitedly as he rushed into the manager's office of Club Illusions.

"I'm surprised he lasted that long," the man laughed. "Who took his spot?

"Ced got the eastside of Decatur now," he replied as he loaded a disk into the DVD. "Security footage from the motel!"

They watched as Robert entered the room but didn't come back out. That explained the second body found. They watched Cameisha and Bad Ass enter the room shortly after. The flash from the gun lit up the window. He got a good look at both faces as they left.

"I'ma put Milsap 'nd 'em on them and..."

"Nah, she'll come to me," he said, nodding in agreement with himself.

****

"This...shit...right...here!" Cameisha proclaimed at a bad ass dress she found in a boutique. She practically ran to the dressing room to try it on.

The short dress was so tight that it squeezed her plump breasts seductively over the top. It hugged her ass so tightly that it made her miss her man. It was perfect, so she set out in search of the perfect shoes to match.

Cameisha could have gone anywhere to get her hair done, but she thought that it would be cute to visit the same salon she'd murdered Mama Salazar in. No one had seen her when she'd slipped inside to slit the wicked woman's throat, so no one would recognize her now. She got a kick out of chopping it up in Spanish with the other woman.

A few hours later, she left with a fresh wash and curl. Most of her liquid locks were pulled into a tasteful bun while two Shirley Temple curls cascaded down to frame her pretty face. She retreated back to her hideout to rest up for her night at the club.

****

"I'm not expecting company," Sherry said to explain why she didn't budge when the doorbell rang.

"Could be your husband," Clarence said, since he now had Robert's keys on his keyring.

Sherry replied with a shrug and kept on watching the movie. It rang once more, followed by an official sounding knock.

"Who?" Sherry demanded as she marched toward the door. Her bouncing butt checks had an audience as she left the room.

"Dekalb County Police!" came the reply through the door.

"I am not paying any bail for anyone," she muttered and opened the door.

"Mrs. Ward?" the detective asked, reading from his notepad.

"Technically," she replied.

"I'm sorry to inform you that your husband, Robert Ward, has passed away. We need a family member to come and make the official identification and claim his remains."

"Um...okay. I'll need a couple of hours, though, if that's okay?"

"Sure. No rush," he replied before handing her the card with the medical examiner's info on it.

"Everything okay?" Clarence asked when she returned.

She sat next to him and cuddled up under him as she had been before the doorbell rang. "Mmhm. My husband dead," she said and took the movie off pause. Clarence frowned down at her nonchalance until she explained. "Babe, my husband died when he left me for dead."

He couldn't argue with that so he turned back to the movie. As soon as the credits began to roll, she stuck her hand down his pants.

She tugged on his dick until it was rock hard and throbbing in her hand. He lifted up to pull his pants down while she stood to step out of hers and mount him.

"I'm all yours now," she said as he inserted himself inside of her. "That's if you want me. Do you want me?"

"Yeah, I do," he assured her while thrusting into her. She rode him fiercely with the dead weight of her husband lifted from her. He shook and grunted as he came but she kept on until she got off, too.

The couple hugged and kissed until the shivers of sex subsided. She pulled her clothes back on without cleaning up, so he did the same. She looked at the address for the coroner's office and nodded.

"I'll drive," he offered when they emerged from the house. There was no telling when the grief would strike and she didn't need to be behind the wheel when it did.

The ride across town was made in total silence. The radio was on but neither paid any attention to it. Once they arrived, he led the way inside and held the door open as she followed.

"I...um...I'm Mrs. Ward. I'm supposed to claim...um...my um..."

"Right this way, ma'am," the sympathetic employee said. He led the couple down a hall and positioned them in front of a window with a drawn curtain. He rushed away so he wouldn't have to hear the grief when the curtain was opened. That was the part of the job that was going to make him quit one day.

"Oh wow!" was all Sherry could say when the curtain was pulled.

Luckily, Clarence was close by when her knees buckled. He caught her and pulled her into his embrace while nodding affirmatively to the medical examiner in the window. All that was left now was putting him in the ground.

Chapter 32

"Nice club," Cameisha remarked as she drove past Club Illusions. She had already been by several times during the day to scope out her escape route, but it looked totally different at night.

The throng of beautiful women stretched down the block made her wish she and her crew were all back together, laughing, dancing and turning down the wannabe players. A sleek black Benz parked in the owner's spot meant it was show time. She'd already parked her getaway car in the back alley, which meant the valet could keep the one she pulled up to the club.

"That thing will hurt you," she shot to the valet trying to steal a peek between her legs as she got out. He settled for the tip she handed him along with her keys.

The valet parking was for VIP so she got in the short line reserved for the so-called Very Important People. There wasn't a teacher, preacher, doctor or scientist amongst them. Society dictated that rappers, athletes, actors and dope boys were more important.

"Welcome to Club Illusions," a burly female bouncer greeted. They dressed her in a cute dress and flats but it was still obvious that she could and would beat a chick up.

"Thank you," Cameisha said and raised her arms to be wanded by the handheld metal detector. It was all good until it passed over her mid-section.

"Um," the bouncer asked when the want beeped at her crotch.

"I got a gun in my coochie!" Meisha spat sarcastically.

"Whatever, but you can't come in until you clear...," she said but stopped when she heard her boss in her ear piece. "Thank you, have fun."

"I will," she said and walked inside. Again, she wished she was there to party when she saw the festive club in full swing. There was a smile on every face except hers. She still couldn't prevent her hips from moving to the music as she moved through the club.

Cameisha tried to climb a bar stool but found it to be uncomfortable so she just posted up next to it. The action was on the dance floor, anyway, where couples dry humped to the latest tunes. Meanwhile, she focused on the office upstairs. King Kong was wearing a nice suit as he blocked the stairway. Her mind scrambled on ways to slip past him so that she could carry out her mission. She gorilla put a finger to his ear to hear the commands in his earpiece. He nodded his head and walked away.

Cameisha took a breath and crept forward. She walked deliberately to the stairs and quickly ascended them. She reached the owner's office and paused. After pressing her ear to the door, she spread her legs and pulled her panties aside to gently remove the loaded pistol.

"Oh wow," she muttered to herself when she went to take it off safety and realized that she'd never put the safety on. Had it gone off inside of her, there would have been no more Dope Girl. "Shoot, if I don't go in here and kill this dude, there won't be no more Dope Girl!"

The pep talk urged her on and she gently turned the door handle. She took a deep breath and eased inside while raising the gun. Her target stood peacefully in front of the window with his arms folded behind his back. A tinge of regret swept through Cameisha's soul. It was fucked up to murder the man like this but he was in her way. Her baby, grandmother and boyfriend would die if he didn't.

"Sorry, no hard feelings," she said and pulled the trigger. The tiny gun barked loudly but didn't bite. She wondered if she'd missed the man who didn't budge. Even with the sound of the gun fired in the room, he didn't move. Cameisha took a few steps closer and fired her last shot. Again, nothing.

"Blanks," he chuckled and slowly turned. Cameisha's eyes went wide and the gun slipped to the floor.

"Daddy?" she blinked rapidly at Cameron Forrest standing before her.

"Yeah, now come give me a hug!" he said, spreading a smile and his arms simultaneously.

"I'm so glad I didn't kill you!" she sobbed in his arms.

"I'm so glad, my nigga Big Shawn put blanks in the gun. Now, tell me. Why are you here? What are you doing?"

"It's a long story," Meisha sighed. They went over to the sofa to be seated so she could lay it all out.

"So why didn't you say something?" he wanted to know at the end of the tale.

"Tell who? They got the phones tapped, froze the bank accounts and keep people at the house..."

"Guess I'll have to go down there and see this Sosa," Cam growled. The thought of his grandmother in danger had him fuming.

"Daddy, ain't no way you can take on all those people alone!" she exclaimed, wide-eyed from fear.

"He's not alone," a voice said, entering the room.

Again, Meisha blinked rapidly trying to focus. The image stayed the same, so she ran over and hugged him. "Uncle Killa!"

Chapter 33

"You sure you don't want me to come? I bust my gun, too. Tell him, Unc!" Cameisha pleaded after Cam laid out the plans.

"She will bust something," Killa replied fondly. "But, he's right."

"Besides, you need to be here when that shipment arrives. Convict and my people will help on that end," Cam explained like the general he was. He was back in the ATL and back on his grind. It put a sparkle in his eyes that made him even more handsome.

"Oh, okay. At least take me to lunch 'fo y'all go," she conceded.

"Fish supreme!" Killa cheered. And who could blame him, that shit is delicious.

****

Killer Cam and Killa needed to stay of the radar literally and figuratively, so they chartered a private jet to fly down to Brazil. They were met by some of Killa's contacts once they landed and whisked away to a safe house.

"Tell us about this Sosa," Cam said once they were settled.

"An animal," Gocho replied, making a face like the name had a bitter taste. "He was supplying the United States through the Salazar family. Unfortunately, they all perished from a suicide bomber at a funeral."

"That was gangsta!" Killa interrupted like a groupie

"Yo, she got that from me! Well, my pops," Cam corrected. Gocho raised his hands and brow as if to ask if he could continue. "My bad, go 'head."

"He somehow linked it to your people and put the press down. He will still kill them all after he gets what he wants. He has no honor!"

"And I have no chill!" Killa added. "Where can we find him?"

"Like you said, a funeral," Cam replied. "Where does his mother live?"

****

"You sure you don't want me to come? My gun bust, too!" Bad Ass assured Cameisha.

"Yeah, I'm sure. My daddy sending his people. If this shit pop off, we're all gonna be rich!"

"Yeah," Self said half-heartedly. His time was up and his family would be gone in days. Angel and Kisha had become close friends so there was no question she was leaving, too.

"Quicker we get this money, the quicker you can bounce," Bad Ass reminded.

"Shit, we can branch out down there, too! My daddy 'bout to have the whole country on lock!" Meisha cheered. Only Bad Ass smiled with her.

Self wasn't moving west to be a dope boy. He was ready to be a husband and a father. Cut grass and grocery shopping. Stuff you can't go to prison for. "Yeah," he repeated but no one believed him. "I'm finna go knock the rest of this work off."

"Finna?!" Bad Ass laughed. "Son, you getting mad country!"

"I ain't said finna!" he shot back.

"Yeah, you did!" Cameisha joined in. "Lil' Mama must got that wet-wet! That shit gave you an accent!"

"Yeah, but I got her saying 'yo' and 'son', so..." he laughed. Not for long, though, because the thought of her leaving was no laughing matter.

****

At eighty-years old, Mrs. Sosa knew she had no damn business driving a car. Not only couldn't she drive, she could barely see. Her thick coke bottle glasses only allowed her to see shapes and colors but nothing more.

"Here she comes," Cam radioed when her Benz left the hilltop gated villa. It was built like a fort, which had kept Killa and Cam at bay. Now, out on the open road, she was fair game.

"I'm on her," Killa replied and pulled out behind her. The road was so crooked and curved, the killer gripped the wheel tightly with both hands.

"You gotta get her before she reaches the town!" Cam warned.

"I know, I know!" he shot back. They both knew if she reached the village, they couldn't get her. They also knew her murder would cause more harm than good. Security would be so tight that they wouldn't be able to get anywhere near her funeral.

That's why she was about to have an accident. Killa took a deep breath like one does before leaping from the high dive. He mashed the gas and pulled up on her bumper.

"Son of a bitch!" the old woman cursed and shook her fist when she felt the bump. Those would be her last words because the next bump sent her barreling off the side of the cliff.

"Dayum!" Cam giggled as he watched the car bounce and flip down the mountain side. It landed in a mangled heap along with several others. Some of the wrecked vehicles still had bodies in them. If relatives couldn't afford to have them retrieved, they were left. The Sosa clan could afford it. That meant a big funeral to send her off in style. Killa-Cam style.

Chapter 34

"What? When? How?" Sosa barked in response to the news of his mother's death. It was good that he received the news via phone so no one could see him pumping his fist in celebration.

He had been waiting patiently for the old lady to die so he could move into the lavish estate. It was fit for the king that he was about to become. He envisioned moving in exotic beauties of all colors and nationalities, Chinese, Indian, Eskimo and Russian. Not to mention the cute little black girl named Cameisha. She would be lonely after he killed off her family.

"I will make all the arrangements," his uncle assured him. "Her remains are safe at the funeral home."

"Yes, handle it. I must go to the villa and take care of things there," Sosa said, meaning move all her shit out of his way.

****

"You probably need to let me handle this part by myself. Just guard the door in case anyone comes," Killa offered once they broke inside the funeral home.

"Shawty, I can handle anything you can handle," Cam shot back. The two had become as close as brothers and just as competitive.

"If you say so," Killa shrugged. He led the way into the morgue where the bodies were kept. The first sheet he lifted revealed a headless corpse. The head was under the sheet as well, but the fingers were missing from both hands.

"Guess he couldn't count," Cameron surmised. In his world, snitches got stitches and thieves lost fingers.

"Damn! Wonder what she did," Killa said when the next lifted sheet revealed a pretty young woman. The ligature marks around her knock suggested she'd been strangled.

"Beats me, but they need to move this funeral up. Dude needs dead," Cam replied.

A round, lumpy mass under the next sheet was that of Mrs. Sosa. Her chest cavity had been sewn up after her organs were removed for autopsy. Killa produced a scalpel from his bag of tricks and cut through the sutures.

"W-w-what are you d-d-doing?" Cam asked, turning green from looking at the woman's insides.

"I t-t-t-told you," he snickered and began stuffing the cavity with explosives. Cam tried to avert his eyes but when he looked down, all he saw was a wrinkled eighty-year-old vagina.

"Damn, that's worse!" he said and looked back up. He watched in muted awe as his cousin hooked wires and blasting caps to the syntax. He could sense the urgency when Killa plugged the wires into a cell phone.

"Whew!" he exclaimed and wiped the sweat from his brow. Attaching a live electrical device to blasting caps is always hit or miss. It's literally do or die. He sewed the body back together and it was time to go. All that was left was the funeral.

****

"How's it looking over there?" Killa asked when Cam took his call. The former was staked out at the funeral home watching family members pile in. The latter was watching their grandmother's house for activity.

"They all left except for one," he replied. Most of the men Sosa had watching the family had left to go pay their respects. Once they got word that the shipment had arrived, they would murder the entire family; the old lady, the kids, the woman and the baby.

"Same here. Err body here except for Sosa. Fuck is this dude?"

"Well, just give me the word," Came said, looking at the cell phone that would trigger the bomb. It was programmed to call the phone inside the dead woman and detonate it.

"Almost ready, just waiting on the guest of...shit!" he replied.

"What? What's happening?" Cam asked urgently.

"They just pulled the carriage around. They'll be moving to the gravesite any minute! Shit, and Sosa hasn't shown yet!"

"What do you want me to do?"

"Blow it! Fuck it, we'll catch him later," Killa replied.

Cam pressed 'send' on the phone and sent the voltage to the blasting caps that detonated the device. He couldn't see, hear or feel it from all the way across town, but it was spectacular.

"Wow!" Killa cheered and clapped like a kid at a fireworks display. No wonder his kids are fucking crazy.

The windows and walls all blew out, raining blood and body parts hundreds of feet. The heavy concrete roof fell in, killing the already dead people again.

"Did it work? What happened?" Cam demanded excitedly. He was happy he'd won the coin toss to pull the trigger but that meant he didn't get to see it.

"Yooooo! That shit was dope!" he giggled

Cameron sprang into action and came out of his hiding spot. The guard parked out front of the Forrest compound frowned when he saw him approaching. He relaxed when he saw the tattered clothing of a beggar. A burlap bag hung from his shoulder to collect trash and trinkets.

"Come!" the man ordered. He gathered up the uneaten sandwich half from lunch to give to him. Little did he know, the man had something for him.

"I don't eat pork," Cameron said. The guard knew he was in trouble when he heard him speak perfect English. He scrambled to pull his gun while Cam watched. Once he had it firmly in hand, he fired.

"What was that?" Sincerity asked Trigga. They both knew they were under siege but had kept it from Grandma Diedra and the kids.

"My grandson is here!" Diedra cheered upon hearing the gunshot.

It was a mystery as to why they thought that the woman who'd raised both Cameron Forrest Sr. and Killa didn't know any better. She knew something was amiss when Cameisha have to go the States all of a sudden. Then there was the strange men lurking about speaking in hushed tones. She also knew that it was just a matter of time until her grandson came and saved the day.

"Cameron, where's Xavier?"

"He had to go to a funeral," he explained and hugged her neck. "He has to make a quick stop by the bank then he'll meet us at the airport. So grab whatever means the most to you and come on!"

Chapter 35

"Where are we going?" Grandma insisted for the hundredth time by the time they reached the airport. Cam was relieved to see Killa arrive so he could answer his questions as well as theirs. He rushed forward to meet him before he reached the family.

"Well?" Cam asked the plethora of questions at once.

"Well, the bank manager agreed to transfer the money. He's left-handed now but the money is safe. One-hundred percent kill rate at the funeral. Still no sign of Sosa," he blurted. The rest would have to wait because the family bum rushed him in greeting.

"Where are we going?" Sincerity asked when she pulled her tongue from Killa's mouth.

"It's not safe here. You're going to Belize," he said in that tone that prevented back talk and protest. They boarded their private plane and taxied on the runway.

Cam smiled down at his namesake while Trigga looked around with his ears. Sincerity held on to little Rico while her older son chatted with Grandma.

"Look at that plane, Grandma," Xavier said, pointing at a private jet lifting off the ground.

"Mmhm, nice," she replied. Except it wasn't nice. It was Sosa headed to Atlanta to meet his shipment.

****

"Just follow our lead. Let me do all the talking," Convict said as he and Cameisha rode over to meet the shipment. He had to convince them that they were going distribute their product. That had been the plan but Cameisha had other plans. That's why her phone had been powered off.

"Un huh," she replied, looking in the car's rearview mirror to see if they were being followed. She cracked a sly smile when she saw that they were.

"You feel that, B?" Self asked as they trailed Convict's truck.

"Feel what?" Bad Ass asked despite feeling the same ominous feeling. He knew Meisha's plan was to double cross the deal was absolutely crazy. She knew that the Sosa clan wouldn't survive a visit from her father and uncle so she planned to keep all the coke for herself. Her father could buy it from her if he wanted it. If not, Self and Bad Ass could move it themselves. As long as they ate, it didn't matter.

"Like, I feel like...we're about to die," he said with a heavy sigh. He had no idea how right he was.

****

"They all die! Every one of them!" Sosa demanded as he briefed his people. He knew immediately that Cameisha was somehow involved in the bombing that killed his family, just like the Salazars. Now he would kill her. She would be dead for real this time. And he'd blow up her funeral. He would just stay in America and set up his own distribution network, despite already being a wanted man.

Sosa wasn't the only one planning. As soon as Cameron touched down in Atlanta, he set his own plans in motion. Cameisha's phone went straight to voicemail but he still had eyes on her since she was riding to the meet with his partner Convict.

Convict frowned at the strange directions on the text. He was a loyal soldier so he shrugged and obeyed. His phone buzzed and he answered with, "Sup, lil' mama?"

"You, Big Daddy," Cameron laughed. Meisha tuned out when she assumed he was talking to some girl. "Change in plans, abort the mission and bring my daughter back to the club."

"Mmm, sounds good. I'm on my way," he replied and mentally changed course.

"W-wha-, where are you going? You missed the exit!" Cameisha protested as they rode past the exit that would take them to the meet.

"Change of plans," he said without even looking in her direction.

"Change in plans! Nigga, you 'bout to blow off a multi-million-dollar deal for some ass?! Shit, I'll give you some ass!" she lied. She would have pulled her gun if he didn't insist she leave it. Now she turned all the way around to see if Self and Bad Ass were still behind them.

"They still there," Convict laughed. He'd been watching them on his tail since they left the club.

"Who? I...aww, shit!" She finally gave up. She crossed her arms and pouted for the rest of the ride back downtown. She figured out that her dad was behind whatever had just happened when they arrived back at the club.

****

"They are here," Sosa's man announced when he saw lights pull up to the warehouse.

"Kill them all!" Sosa shot back. His men puffed their chests and cocked the guns but still were not ready. A moment later, all hell broke loose.

"POLICE!!!" the first of many shouted as they barged through the door.

They were met with gunfire and immediately returned fire. More cops came swinging in through the windows on ropes like Batman. Flash and stun grenades filled the night with shock and awe. The gun battle raged for several minutes before coming to a deadly end.

"Shit!" Sosa fussed as he listened to automatic gunfire on the phone. He shook his head at the loss of his men but still wore a smile on his face.

****

"Come on," Convict demanded when they reached the club. He marched quickly, forcing Cameisha to have to jog to keep up. Once he deposited her in the boss' office, he went back for her partners in crime. "Come on!"

"Us?" Little Self asked as if there was someone else in the car he could be talking to. It was a silly question so Convict didn't even bother to answer it. He led the teens up to the office and let them wait with their boss until his boss returned. An hour, although it seemed much longer, passed before the door opened and in walked Cam.

"Daddy, I-"

"Daddy, nothing!" Cam shot back and shut her up. He picked up the remote and aimed it at the flat screen that dominated one of the walls. The nightly news had just come on and they were the top story.

"Acting on a tip, police raided a Southside warehouse. A massive gun battle ensued and claimed the lives of two police officers as well as ten suspects. The target, Roberto Sosa, was not found and no narcotics were recovered..."

"No drugs! Where is Sosa? I thought you..." Cameisha fussed.

"DON'T THINK!" Cam shouted at her then turned to Self and Bad Ass. "And you two were going to rob them? With a Mac and a Chopper."

The two lowered their heads as they were laughed at. Self realized how close he'd come to losing his girl, his daughter and his life. At that moment, he was done. He would flip burgers or bag groceries if he had to. No more dope boy.

"BACK TO YOU, YOU...YOU SELFISH LITTLE BRAT! DO YOU SEE HOW MUCH TROUBLE YOU CAUSED WITH YOUR SHIT?" Cam shouted hotly. Cameisha opened her mouth to make excuses but got cut off once more. "NO, NO MORE TALKING! I'm taking you to the airport personally. Killa will meet your flight and take you home. DON'T COME BACK..."

"Okay," she whined. "But what about my money? What about Aqua? What about my brothers?"

"The money is straight. You got a cool million waiting on you."

"A million?! I had eight!" she protested.

"And now you got one! I'll take care of these guys and send your girl down there with you. But, this is the end...no more dope girl!"

The End.

Epilogue

Well, Cameisha pouted the whole way to Belize, but got right once she saw her baby. I sent her friend Aqua and her son down there to live as well.

I would love to meet her friend Samantha, but that's another story.

I set Self and Bad Ass up down in Houston. Bought them both starter houses and bankrolled their business idea. Made them change the name to 'Bad-Self Beauty and Barbershop'. I even sprang for Kisha's operation. She had movement in her feet but couldn't try walking until she gives birth. I sure hoped those two stay straight.

Me, I was back in my city where I belonged. The king was back and I was ready to take back my throne! Get ready, World, it's the Return of the Dope Boy!

www.ingramcontent.com/pod-product-compliance
Lightning Source LLC
Chambersburg PA
CBHW011718240626
47153CB00009B/2907
* 9 7 8 1 9 5 2 5 4 1 9 9 5 *